LESSONS IN LOVE

1963. Lucy's first teaching job turns out to be more than she bargained for . . . fired with enthusiasm to show her teaching skills, she is brought down to earth when she faces a depressing room and difficult pupils. However, her mum is always there for her and she soon begins to find herself with an increasingly complicated love life. Who should she choose to spend time with? And why is the Headmaster so concerned about the company she keeps?

CHRISSIE LOVEDAY

LESSONS IN LOVE

Complete and Unabridged

LINFORD
Leicester

First published in Great Britain in 2008

First Linford Edition
published 2009

British Library CIP Data

Loveday, Chrissie
    Lessons in love.—Large print ed.—
Linford romance library
    1. Love stories
    2. Large type books
    I. Title
    823.9'2 [F]

    ISBN 978–1–84782–604–6

Published by
F. A. Thorpe (Publishing)
Anstey, Leicestershire

Set by Words & Graphics Ltd.
Anstey, Leicestershire
Printed and bound in Great Britain by
T. J. International Ltd., Padstow, Cornwall

This book is printed on acid-free paper

Visit the author's website at:
www.chrissieloveday.com

1

'I can't believe we're virtually trained teachers,' Lucy said happily as she and her best friend, Anne, stood on the station platform.

'And we've both got jobs,' Anne agreed.

It was the end of their college lives together. Three years of hard work starting in 1960, plenty of heartache, lots of fun and companionship and now it was all over.

'Responsibilities. Careers and whatever happens next,' Lucy said cheerfully. 'And this is only the start of the sixties, when anything and everything could happen. Don't you sense this is the start of something big?'

'Maybe. Yes, of course it is. But frankly, at this point in time, I'm so shattered, all I want to do is veg out.' Anne closed her eyes as if she was about to fall asleep.

'I guess so. That final party was exactly that. The end of it all. I'm still getting over it. Give us a couple of weeks though and we'll be ready for anything. I think this is my train coming. I'll see you in a couple of weeks.'

She was really looking forward to a lazy time being looked after by her mum. It wasn't quite the end as they would be meeting at another friend's wedding. Sarah and her fiancé had decided to marry as soon as possible after leaving college and everyone in their year was invited.

'Bye, love. Have a good journey. Mine's due in about ten minutes. I can't believe this really is it for us.'

'See you soon.' Lucy hauled her large suitcase and seemingly endless bags into the carriage. Some of her friends just didn't know how lucky they were to have parents with cars who collected them with three years' worth of possessions to shift. As it was, Lucy had sent her old trunk on ahead of her with all the books, files and as much heavy stuff as she could cram in. She flopped down in the last empty seat and smiled apologetically at the other occupants as she piled her things around her.

As the city of Birchester was left behind her, she watched the green fields flashing past the train's windows. She could hardly believe that three years could go by so fast. She had gone straight to the Domestic Science College after her A levels and now, at twenty-two, was all ready to begin her new life. She was fortunate to have found a job in her old home town teaching Home Economics.

She planned to live at home for a while and then maybe she could save up for her own place. She knew how much her widowed mother would enjoy spoiling her and they could spend time together again, just as they had when she was in the sixth form. Her years away at college had been difficult for her mother, she knew, but that was over now. She almost dozed as the miles were eaten up by the train.

The rhythm of the wheels fitted into her slumber and before she realised it, she had reached the station. She gathered her belongings and heaved them across to the next platform where she could catch a connecting train to her local station. She hoped her mum would have walked along the path to meet her as the thought of the long walk down the lane with both hands and arms full was quite a daunting prospect.

'Always the longest bit, isn't it?' the lady sitting next to her said. 'Been away, have you?'

'I'm going home after college. I've just finished so there's tons of stuff to bring back. And I threw away quite a lot,' she added ruefully.

'It's Lucy, isn't it? Lucy Hodges?'

'Well yes. I'm sorry . . . ?'

'Maisie Stonewall. I live down the lane before yours. I know your mum,

4

Sylvia. Used to go to school together we did. I remember when you were just a little slip of a thing. I passed on some of my Josie's clothes to your mum, during the war.'

'Oh yes, of course. Mrs Stonewall. Sorry, I didn't recognise you. Think I'm half asleep actually.'

'This is it, our station. Don't know what we'd do without our local trains. Well, have a nice holiday. We'll catch up sometime. Our Josie will be interested to hear I've met you. She's got one little one and another on the way already. Can't believe it.'

'I'm sure you can't,' Lucy replied automatically. Her Josie couldn't be much older than she was. A year or so maybe and she was already a mum, almost twice over. Scary, Lucy thought.

'Oh, there's Mum,' she said. 'Mum . . . over here. Oh it's lovely to see you.' She dragged her parcels and suitcase out of the train and let them fall in a heap on the platform and she hugged Sylvia.

'You look tired, love,' her mother greeted her. 'And thin. You've lost some weight. Never mind, a few days of home cooking and we'll soon have you looking better. Now, is this everything?' Together, mother and daughter walked out of the station. Lucy handed over her ticket and the station-master smiled at Sylvia.

'Got her back then,' he said as he waved them through.

'That's right. Thanks for letting me on without a platform ticket.'

'No problem, but don't tell everyone or I'll be losing my job. All right then, Lucy? I know your mum's been looking forward to having you home.'

'I'm looking forward to a break. Then you'll be seeing me every day when I travel into Longridge. I'll be teaching at The Mount in September. Nice and near the station.'

'Eh, our little Lucy a teacher,' the station-master said with a grin. 'I remember your mum bringing you to watch the trains when you were still in your pram. Where does time go to?'

The next few days seemed to be filled with reminiscences every time they went outside the door. Life in the Potteries seemed to have a slower pace than in the larger, anonymous town she had become used to for the past three years. Here, everyone had time to stop and chat and as everyone knew everything else, there was plenty to catch up on.

At the end of the first week, Lucy began to long to go out to somewhere where nobody knew her. If things didn't change, it was going to be stifling to stay at home all the time. Most of her old, real friends had either lost touch or had moved away themselves. Still, another week and she would be meeting her college friends at Sarah's wedding. Although she was really looking forward to it, there might be one problem looming. Alistair.

He was a friend of Sarah's fiancé and of course, was invited to the wedding. Lucy and Alistair had been an item for almost two years. It had started when a crowd of the girls from her own college had met up with a crowd of boys from the all male college nearby. Several of them, including Sarah and Graham, had paired off and though they often went out together in a noisy, fun seeking gang, they also had their quiet moments when just the two of them were together. Gradually, Lucy had realised that they weren't going anywhere and had finished with Alistair.

'You can't mean it?' he had protested. 'I thought we were rubbing along nicely together.'

'That's just it, Alistair. We're rubbing along, as you put it. Being here in Birchester is the only thing we really have in common.'

'But I . . . I think I might be close to . . . well, being in love with you. Wow. I've said it. The 'L' word.'

'If you only think you might be close, then it shouldn't matter so much. If you really were in love with me, it would be so much worse. I'm sorry. We've had fun, but I really have to concentrate on my finals.'

'But after that? I was going to ask you if you'd like to go to France with me. With the family, I mean. Mum and Dad have booked a chalet place for a couple of weeks and there's plenty of room.'

It sounded amazing and very tempting, but Lucy knew it would be a mistake. Besides, her mum would be most disappointed if she went away for so much of the holiday.

'It would have been great, but I really can't. Thank you for asking me. I'm sorry, Alistair, but I really can't see a future for us.'

That had been over two months ago. He had written to her twice and even sent flowers on the day of her first final exam. She had sent him a polite note of thanks, but had stuck to her decision. Now she had to face him again at Sarah's wedding.

'So, what are you going to wear for the wedding?' her mother asked.

'Haven't decided yet. I'll have to

make do with whatever's in my wardrobe. I can't afford to buy anything new.'

'You must have a hat though. Everyone wears hats at a wedding.'

'I still can't afford it.'

'Well, maybe we should go shopping tomorrow. I've a bit put by and we can choose a nice hat and if it's not too expensive, a dress to go with it?'

'Oh, Mum, that's very sweet of you, but I couldn't.'

'Nonsense. It would be my pleasure. You'll be earning money very soon and contributing to the expenses. If I can't treat my only daughter to a nice outfit, well, it's a poor do.' Lucy stared at her mum and wondered when was the last time she'd bought herself anything new. She gave her a hug and felt tears pricking her eyes.

'You're much too good to me. Supporting me for three years even after all the time at school.'

'You got a good grant. You've never asked for any extras as many students do. I'm proud of how you've managed your budget over the years.'

'Well, I am supposed to be a Home Economist. But thanks, Mum. You're the best. I really mean it.'

'And you need to look your best. They'll all be dressed up in their finery. And I expect that Alistair will be there, won't he?'

'Yep. He certainly will.' She'd told her mother about their break-up and how he'd taken it badly.

'Well, there you are. You don't want him thinking you're moping.'

'But I'm not. I was the one who finished it. I'm fine about it. He may be rolling in family money, but that's nothing if you don't truly love the person. Well, is it?'

'Course not. I'm still very proud of you, for even knowing all that at your age. Your dad would have been proud too. You've turned into a lovely young woman. On the inside as well as the outside.'

Lucy smiled and thought about her

own father. He had died when she was quite small and she scarcely remembered him. She and her mother had formed a very close bond as a result and were good friends. She was proud of that and could never understand when her friends complained about their own families, as many seemed to do.

'Thanks, Mum. OK then. Hanley tomorrow? If I don't buy an actual outfit, maybe some nice fabric and I can make something.'

'You'll only have a few days. Can you do it in the time?'

'Course I can. I've been known to buy a remnant from the market on a Saturday morning and wear the new dress to a party in the evening.'

'Goodness. But then, I suppose you've been trained for it.'

'Not sure my needlework lecturers would always approve of the neatness of the finish, but it usually looked good.'

They caught the early bus from the end of the lane on the Monday morning and had a wonderful time browsing through stacks of fabrics in the big shops. They both fell in love with a delicate pale blue linen with a fine tracery of flowers in a darker blue.

'That's just gorgeous. If we can only find a blue hat to go with it, you'll look a picture. Bring out the blue in your eyes.'

'It's expensive though. Almost ten shillings a yard. I'd need at least three yards and then there's all the extras. Buttons, zip, tailor's canvas and thread.'

'And a pattern.'

'I can manage without. I've got a basic bodice block and skirts are easy enough. I was thinking though, it would be nice if I made a sleeveless dress and a jacket. Then I could take off the jacket for the evening dancing.'

'Whatever you like, love. It's hardly the expensive outfit I was planning. Best get four yards and then you'll be sure. And stop worrying about the expense. It will be a useful outfit to have in your wardrobe.'

They made their purchases and even added lining for the jacket. They went along to C&As to look for a hat. There was always a good selection there. In fact, one of the favourite Saturday morning activities in Birchester had been to go and try on hats in their local branch. They giggled at some of the more exotic designs and a cross looking assistant came and stood close by, glaring at the pair.

'Are you looking for something in particular?' she snapped when she could stand it no longer.

'A blue straw hat with a wide brim. But you don't seem to have anything suitable,' Lucy said primly.

'Perhaps the one your sister is holding is quite near your request.'

'My sister?' Lucy squeaked. She looked at her mother and laughed again. Her face softened into a smile. Actually, her mother was quite young looking and the assistant wasn't being ridiculous. 'No. It isn't quite right. Not the right shade of blue. We'll try somewhere else, thank you.'

'Your sister?' laughed her mother as they left the shop. 'Why didn't you put her right?'

'Cos you're gorgeous. You could easily be my sister and I can't think why I hadn't noticed it before.'

'Because I'm your mum. I stopped being Sylvia Hodges and became your mum the day you were born. I've been known as Lucy's mum ever since.'

'Then it's time you were Sylvia Hodges again. Person in your own right. Let's get this wedding over and we'll start sorting you out. Time to live a little.'

'That sounds quite scary. My own daughter sorting me out, as you put it.' All the same, she was blushing slightly and looked pleased.

Lucy tucked her arm into her mother's, rearranged the shopping bags and together they set off for the next store. It was one o'clock before they had finished. A handbag and shoes, both reduced in the end of season sale, had been added to their purchases.

'I think we should have a bite to eat in the cafeteria. Save us cooking when we get back and anyhow, I'm quite exhausted and in need of a sit down.'

'Sounds great, but you've spent a fortune on me already today. Thanks again, Mum. I'm really looking forward to getting the sewing machine out.'

'I think we've done pretty well actually. The whole rigout for just over a tenner. You've become quite a bargain hunter haven't you?'

'After being a student for three years, it's a case of dire necessity. Anyway, those shoes were an absolute bargain. You're sure the hat's OK? It's really only a sunhat but it does the job, doesn't it?'

'If you put a band of the dress material round it, it'll look brilliant. Nobody will ever know. Come on. I fancy some fish and chips. What do you want?'

They sat at the brightly-coloured table in the brightly-coloured cafeteria and munched their meal. They had a pot of tea and slices of bread and butter to go with it.

'They call this butter?' Sylvia moaned. 'It's marg, if I'm not mistaken. You'd think they'd manage best butter at these prices.' Lucy stifled a grin. As long as she could remember this had been her mother's comment whenever they ate out. 'Can't say I like this decor very much,' she added, nodding at the walls. 'Too busy.'

'They design these patterns everywhere to get people in and out as fast as possible. Not meant to be restful. That way, there's always room for people to sit and eat.'

'Never thought of that. Clever, I s'pose.'

'We spent a day working on a cafeteria when I was at college. Part of my education. Actually, we were pleasantly surprised at the quality of the ingredients. Now, hadn't we better move or we'll miss the next bus?'

Lucy spent the next couple of days

working at the old sewing machine. It was an old hand machine and very different to the modern electric ones she had been used to using at college.

'One of the first things I'm getting is a new electric machine,' she said at the end of the day when her arms felt as if they'd drop off.

'You're making a lovely job of that outfit,' Sylvia told her. 'My word, you're as good as anyone could want. Maybe that's something you could do in your spare time. Take in sewing.'

'I suspect I'm going to be very busy in the next few months. It's a daunting task starting teaching. There. Just need to press it and I'm done.'

After supper, she tried on the whole ensemble.

'You look gorgeous, Lucy. Very well worth the effort. You'll be the belle of the ball, next to the bride of course. It's just that . . . well isn't the skirt a bit short?'

2

Confident in her new finery, Lucy went into the church with Anne and Anne's brother, Joe, who had driven them both to the wedding. It was a perfect summer's day and they were all looking forward to seeing their friends safely married. The small church was packed and as the newcomers looked, there seemed to be a sea of brightly coloured hats and shimmering outfits.

'Wow, it all looks a bit posh, doesn't it?' muttered Anne. 'I'm glad I borrowed one of Mum's hats or I'd be right out of it. You look great, by the way. New outfit? Well it must be cos I haven't seen it before.'

'There's the rest of the gang, over there. Shall we see if we can fit in the same pew?' Lucy hesitated as she spotted Alistair. He was sitting next to a petite red-head who wore a tiny fluff of a creation on her head.

'Isn't that . . . ?'

'Yes.' Lucy smiled and linked arms with Anne and her brother, Joe.

'What is she wearing? The woman with him?'

'I believe it might be called a hat. Or nearly.' They giggled as they moved towards the front of the church. They scrambled along the pew in front of Alistair to join several of their other friends. They greeted each other in a flurry of loud whispers.

'Graham's looking nervous. That's his brother as best man, isn't it?'

'Rather dishy.'

'Hands off. He's married and even has a child.'

'You're looking a bit swish. Love the hat.'

'Thanks,' Lucy replied happily.

She was enjoying herself. It was good to be among her friends and enjoy the banter once more. The organ struck a chord and everyone shushed each other. All eyes turned towards the back of the church as Sarah entered. A ripple of sighs went around as people saw the vision of white lace walking down the aisle.

'Doesn't she look just gorgeous?' muttered Anne.

'She is gorgeous, but especially so today. She was right about the dress, though. It's sensational.' They'd all heard every detail about it for the last two months and now, seeing it in all its glory for the first time, couldn't fault her choice. The females in the group felt moved to tears. The males said things like, 'lucky old Graham'. When the service was over and seemingly hours spent on taking photographs, they finally went on to the hotel for the reception. It was all quite grand . . . much more so than any of them had been expecting.

'This must be costing her parents a bomb,' Lucy exclaimed. 'The flowers alone must fill at least half a florist's shop.'

'She never let on that she came from

such a wealthy background, did she?'

'That's Sarah for you.'

'Hello, Lucy,' said a voice from behind her and she turned as she felt a tap on the shoulder. 'Can I introduce Myra? Friend of mine.' Alistair stood looking smug as Myra hung on to his arm and looked up adoringly at him.

'Pleased to meet you,' Lucy said politely. 'Have you known Alistair for long?'

'One whole week. It's our anniversary . . . or whatever you call a week long anniversary.' She spoke in slightly childish sounding voice and Lucy was almost inclined to laugh. Instead, she continued to smile and made nice comments about the wedding. Alistair was staring at her as if he didn't know what to say. Clearly he had hoped to make her jealous but if she was, she certainly didn't show it. Joe joined them and put a hand under Lucy's elbow.

'I think we're supposed to be taking our seats at the tables,' he said. 'You're next to me and the rest of the gang are all close to us. Should be fun. Excuse us, won't you?' He gently led her away and left Alistair looking slightly put out. Myra cuddled close to him and he began to look at her with some distaste.

'Hadn't we better find our seats?' Myra asked, still gazing adoringly at Alistair. He led her to join some of his own college group.

It had been a wonderful day and once the bride and groom had been sent on their way, all the guests began to drift away too. Lucy had spent much of the evening dancing with Joe and had been pleased to have someone to be with, so that Alistair wouldn't think she was moping without him. She was spending the night with Anne and her family and then Joe was driving her back the next day, after lunch.

He lived a little further away, but it was more or less on his route home.

'It's been nice to meet you,' Joe told her as he dropped her off at her mother's house. 'Perhaps you'd like to go out sometime?'

'What, you and I?' she asked incredulous. Joe was at least five years older than her and according to Anne, had girlfriends in every town around. 'It's a bit far for us to meet regularly. I mean to say, you hardly want an hour-and-a-half drive just to go out for a drink or the cinema.'

'You seemed happy enough being with me last night when we were dancing together.'

She blushed slightly, remembering how he had held her close during the last waltz. She certainly hadn't minded then but surely, he was much too old for her?

'I'll give you a call sometime. What's your number?'

'I'm afraid we don't have a phone.'

'Oh. I see. Well, I'll give you my number and maybe you can give me a call? I hope so.'

'Thanks very much for driving me home. I enjoyed everything. Lovely weekend.'

'No problem. And don't forget to

call. I'll be waiting to hear from you.' He waved as he drove away and Lucy couldn't help but smile. He's nice, she thought and turned to go into the house.

'Come and tell me all about it,' her mother insisted. 'Every detail. I've got the kettle boiled and we can sit down with a nice cup of tea while you tell me.'

All too soon the holiday was drawing to a close. Lucy's contract with her new school began on September the first. She felt nervous but excited. She had not even visited the school as she had been appointed by the county advisor following her interview at the City offices. All she knew was that there was another Home Economics teacher who worked in the second specialist room, but she was a part timer and very much older than her.

Lucy felt distinctly unprepared as she went into the school building that first morning of term. There was a brief staff meeting to introduce new members of the team and then it was in at the deep end. She was handed a bunch of keys and told it must be left in the office each evening. She also took a register and a bundle of papers with the school rules and she was dispatched to her room.

'Ian will explain everything to you. He teaches woodwork in the room next to yours. Being on a split site, you are responsible for collecting your students and crossing them over the road,' the Head told her. 'You won't have any students this morning as we are conducting tutorial sessions and you won't have your own group at first. We try not to give a form to you people over the road as it makes for a few complexities. But, there may be occasions when staff are absent and you will be required to cover for them. Any questions?'

'I expect there will be hundreds when it comes to it, but nothing I can think of at present. Thank you.'

'Fine. Introduce yourself to Ian and

I'm sure he'll help all he can. Woodwork and Home Economics usually seem to go together.'

She left the Head's office and went into the little, rather crowded staff room. She hesitated. Who on earth was Ian?

'Hello, love. Finding your way around? I'm Gary. Gary Pritchard, Geography,' he added as if that explained everything.

'Lucy. Lucy Hodges. Home Economics.' She felt slightly ridiculous, but so nervous that she could only repeat his introduction. 'Erm . . . can you tell me which one's Ian?'

'That's him. The slightly better looking chap by the window. Here, Ian. Young lady to see you.' The man glanced up at Gary, and rose to his feet as he saw Lucy standing beside him.

Lucy felt her heart give a slight flutter, not only at meeting a colleague but there was something about his easy grace as he strode across the room. He was tall and had blond curly hair and the clearest blue eyes she had ever seen. He stuck out a hand and grinned.

'Whatever he's told you about me isn't true. You must be our new lady cook.'

'I guess I am. Though I like to think of myself as a bit more than just a cook.'

'Sure you do. And I can wield more than a screwdriver. We're the outcasts who are banished over the road. But, we can usually manage to have a bit of life over there. As long as we can sort out the coffee at break and occasional cream cakes from the bakery, we shall get along just fine. Wednesdays and Fridays, they produce the most wonderful cream fruit pies. We take turns in buying them and we have our own coffee fund. Oh and if you can't make use of any cooking you demonstrate, I can always help out.'

'Just ignore him, love. He thinks only of his stomach. Any trouble with him and you come to me,' Gary told her.

'You're very kind, but I'm quite a

tough lady. After three years at my college, you have to be. So, are you going to show me the way over to this room of mine? I hadn't realised it was actually away from the school itself. Isn't that all very inconvenient?'

'Pluses and minuses. Very convenient for some things but irritating when it's raining and we have to cross the road. But we manage. And we're pretty well left to our own devices. Most of the time. Bit far for the Head to venture out. Mind you, I expect we'll get visits from the powers that be quite often, to start with. You being a probationer and all that. OK then. Got everything you need? We'll make our pilgrimage to the wild blue yonder that calls itself the craft blocks.'

Lucy wondered about this man with whom she was about to be thrown together. He was gorgeous and she would bet most of the girls thought so too. She looked for a ring, but he didn't wear one. Still, that meant absolutely nothing. Not all men wore a wedding ring. She could hardly ask him personal questions so soon. All the same, it might be nice to know his background or at least, something about it.

'Do you live in Longridge?' she asked.

'No. Out at Blythe. Not too far. I've got a car too, so that helps. Decided it was the first thing I'd get hold of when I started earning a regular wage. You?'

'Laston. I'm quite near the station so it's an easy journey. Can't imagine I'll ever afford a car. I'm living with my mum at the moment.'

'That'll help with the savings. Right now. The kids usually line up here and we both see them over the road. Usually, one of us stands in the road and the other waits till they've all gone. Then it's along this passageway and over there's your room and mine's back there. Marion's room is the bigger one over the other side of the playground.'

'Not exactly what you could call compact and convenient. Well, thanks anyhow. I'll take a look inside and see what I make of it all.'

'Hope Bill's lit the stove. It's like an ice box in there, even in summer. Cheerio. See you later.'

Lucy unlocked the door and went into her new domain. Her heart sank. It was a dark and rather depressing room with very ancient looking equipment. There was no fire burning to take off the chill. There were several small kitchen units, standing in rows down the room and two sinks at the back, one of which had an electric water heater. A huge cupboard housed a collection of tubs and jars for ingredients and a selection of baking tins.

As she explored the room, she found some of the things she would need, but everything looked grubby and neglected. Clearly, her first lessons would be spent in showing the pupils how to clean various pieces of equipment. Either that, or she would be spending hours doing it herself. How could anyone have left things in this state?

She opened an oven door and saw

that it too was pretty mucky. There was an elderly washing machine and a drying rack, so at least the tea towels and dishcloths could be washed. This was going to prove quite a challenge after some of the wonderful rooms she had been in for her teaching practice, not to mention all the state of the art college rooms.

She put a kettle on to boil. Maybe there was some coffee somewhere. A knock sounded at the door and Ian came in.

'You managing?'

'Well, I've just decided the first tasks are to do a thorough spring clean. What's been going on over here? Everything's in a dreadful state and the range of equipment's pretty poor.'

'The last teacher had a . . . well, she left when she became ill.'

'She had a what, were you going to say?'

'Oh well. Someone's going to tell you before long. She had a nervous breakdown. Couldn't cope and left in a hurry. They hadn't been able to find a replacement till you breezed along.'

'Heavens. I'm not surprised. State of this place. And what about Marion, did you say her name was?'

'She's part time. The other room's much better than this, but she's been there forever. You'll never get your hands on that room. Even if she is only using it part of the week. Anyhow, I come bearing gifts. I bring coffee and chocolate biscuits. Even got some milk. How are you fixed for a quick break?'

'Wonderful. Kettle's just boiled.' Even if the room was awful, this job was going to have it's compensations. 'So when is Marion due in? We shall have to discuss syllabus and everything. I'm a bit in the dark about what to do.'

'You poor soul. You have been thrown in at the deep end.'

'I'm just wondering how best to get things cleaned up. It hardly seems fair on the kids to ask them to do it, first lesson.'

'Would you like me to see the Head

with you? Maybe we can get some cleaner type to help. You shouldn't have to spend your own time doing it.'

'There's not even any hot water.'

'Ah, do remember that the first job each day is to switch it on at the cylinder. But you need to turn it off at night as it could be a fire hazard. And there's a gas heater you have to switch on and light the pilot light. Now come on. Coffee will make you feel a bit better.'

The more Lucy looked, the worse it all seemed. However would she remember all these tasks? There was a store room at the back that might once have been used as a dining-room of sorts, but it was too piled up with unusable rubbish and what looked like first quality junk. She felt near to tears by the time she reached lunch. She had brought a packed lunch for the first day, not knowing what was available. She munched her sandwiches and once more, Ian came to join her.

'You look upset. Is everything OK?'

'Not really. I just wish I could have seen this place before today. Why couldn't I have been shown around before now?'

'You might not have come back. Anyway, you'd never get people to come in before term starts. Against all the union rules I guess.'

'I'm really going to have to see the Head. I can't cook in a place like this. It's unhygienic for a start.'

Lucy and Ian walked their group of first years across after lunch. They seemed small and eager and she thought maybe it wasn't going to be so bad after all.

They all sat down quietly and she introduced herself and began to explain about their course. She was going to begin with some basic hygiene rules and then suggest they might do a little bit of cleaning to start with. She could teach them how she wanted them to wash up.

'This room's rubbish. My mum wouldn't want me to be doing all this sort of stuff,' one little girl announced firmly.

'It's not fair you should expect us to do your work for you,' said another.

Good grief Lucy thought. It first years are like this, how on earth will I cope with the older kids? Fourth and fifth years were notoriously stroppy and here she was, failing at the first hurdle.

'Fair enough,' she said. The two girls who had spoken stared back at her. They hadn't expected to win so easily. The others looked around at each other and began to grin. This one was going to be easy. Lucy continued. 'I agree. It isn't fair that you should do my work. Nor is it fair that I do your work when the time comes. So, let's agree right now that anything you use or make dirty will be left absolutely spotless so I'll never have any complaints from the next class who come in. Is that fair?'

There were mutters of 'yes miss'.

'So, if I get everything in here really clean before you come again, there will never be any cries of not fair again?'

They looked at each other.

'Please, Miss, did someone else leave the room this dirty?'

'Yes, they did. I'm a new teacher here and this is also my first day. Just like you. I was very shocked to see how dirty everything is and I haven't had any time yet to make things how I want them to be.'

'I don't mind helping you out, Miss,' said the little girl who had first objected.

'Yer, we'll all help won't we?'

Lucy could have cried in relief. The rest of the afternoon was spent in a buzz of activity. With all twenty of the girls helping, and a great deal of noise, the room began to improve a little. Drawers were cleaned out and cutlery washed. She began to realise the benefits of working away from anyone else's classroom, but that she would have to quell the noise in future. She could never work with this racket. Surprisingly quickly, the afternoon passed and it was going home time. Ian popped in as he was leaving.

'How did it go?'

'All right, after a rocky start.'

'Looks better all ready. I take it they co-operated?'

'A bit. But it will take more than a group of first years to bring this round. I'm going to see the Head now. Something has to be done.'

'Good luck. See you tomorrow.' He swung out of the room and blew her a kiss. Her heart leapt. Maybe not everything was bad about this place.

3

The Head was not available. Lucy went home clutching her timetable and desperately trying to work out what she would do the following day. Practical cookery would not happen this week so she had three more days to attempt to organise the room. She made a decision. If the Head was unable to help, she planned to contact the advisor and get some help. She may be new at the game and a lowly probationary teacher, but there was no way she could work in such conditions and produce the high standard of work she was hoping for. Her mother was quite upset by the story Lucy told her.

'You're right, love. You simply must get someone to help sort things out. That's not what you're being paid for. I'd come in with you myself, but I suppose that's not on. What are the rest of the staff like?'

'Haven't seen much of anyone. The woodwork teacher is OK. He and I look as if we'll be working together quite a bit as we're in this separate building over a road.'

'Tell me about him?'

'He is in his twenties, I should think. Quite tall with amazing blue eyes. Blond curly hair. Lives at Blythe.'

'And you quite like him, I gather.'

'I suppose so. Hardly know him really but we did have a coffee together. And lunch.' Sylvia smiled and looked knowingly at her daughter. 'And what's that look for, Mum? No, he's not my type. Stop looking at me like that.'

'I'm not. Now, supper won't be long. Have you got any homework?'

'I'm a teacher now, Mum, not a pupil. I'm the one who sets the homework, remember?'

'I meant have you got any work to do. P'raps you'd like to make a start before we eat.'

'I just want to collapse in a chair and

reflect on the stupid idiot I am to make a commitment without even seeing the place first. Did I say, the previous teacher had a nervous breakdown? That's why everything's such a mess.'

'Well, I hope that's not going to happen to you. Just you stick out for what you want. Don't let it grind you down.'

'Mind if I put the radio on? I want to hear some Beatles music or something. Cheer me up. I won't have it too loud,' she promised, knowing how much her mother disliked the noisier sounds of today's pop groups.

'There's a letter for you on the side. Sorry, I'd forgotten.'

Lucy stared at the postmark and didn't recognise the handwriting. She tore it open, curious to know who'd written to her. It was from Joe. Her eyes widened in surprise.

Dear Lucy,
Just wanted to wish you all the best for your new job. Had hoped you'd

call me by now to arrange that evening out. What about it? Anne assures me you have no ties currently. I'm quite a reliable sort of chap really, whatever my little sister might have said to warn you off. Maybe you'd like to go to a dance . . . there are some good bands playing locally. How about Trentham Gardens one Saturday? Please give me a ring.

Best wishes, Joe. xx

'Anything interesting, dear?' her mother called.

'It's from Joe. He's asked me out again. Can't think why he'd be interested in me. I'm loads younger than him and well, he's rather dishy, so he can't exactly be short of someone to take out.'

'Will you go?'

'I'm not sure. I suppose it might be fun. He was wishing me well for my first day. Wonder how the others are getting on? Bet none of them have quite the horrors of The Mount to cope with.'

She didn't sleep much that night and

when she did wake, felt a muzzy headache coming on. She caught the early train and was ready to begin her battles. Once more, the Head was unavailable and she felt angry. It was almost as if he were avoiding her deliberately. She told his secretary that she needed to see him urgently and told her that she was about to phone the County Advisor. The secretary blinked.

'Oh, I don't think you can do that. Not without reference to the Head.'

'Well, I'm sorry, but if he isn't ever available to see me and this is very urgent, I have no alternative. Perhaps you'll pass on that information. Count this as my reference to the Head.' She turned and went out of the office, shutting the door slightly more firmly than she'd intended.

'Steady on there,' Gary said as she almost ran into him. 'Is there something wrong?'

'There certainly is. I am appointed here as a teacher and not a cleaner. That room over there is quite unusable and until something is done about it, then I require alternative accommodation.'

'Wow. You're certainly not the little scared probationer we were expecting. Good for you, lassie. I was going to tell you that Marion is in today and she might be able to help you. But it seems you don't need a lot of help.'

'I need all the help I can get, actually. Especially in getting someone who can get things done.'

'I understand you wish to see me,' boomed a voice behind her. It was the Head himself looking rather annoyed. 'Perhaps you'd better come into my office, Miss Hodges. I should tell you that I'm not accustomed to having my secretary bullied or spoken to the way you have done.'

'Well then, I must apologise, but I have to say that I have been treated rather shabbily. Naturally I was angry myself. I tried to see you yesterday but you were unavailable and again today when I asked. I came in early to try to sort something out. I don't know if you have been in my room recently, but it really isn't fit for anyone to use. Let alone teach cookery.'

'Miss Jenkins was there for years and she never complained.'

'Maybe not. But I understand she left in well, rather a hurry. The room has been left dirty, ill-equipped and frankly, downright dismal.'

'Get the girls to clean it up. It's all part of the subject, isn't it?'

'Some of the first years had a bit of a go yesterday. Made a start if you like, to put it that way. But I don't see why they should have to clean up someone else's mess. I need a team of cleaners in there and a load of new equipment.'

'Miss Hodges. I resent your tone. You are a new member of staff here and a probationer to boot. It's all part and parcel of teaching these days. You must learn to make the best of it. Yes, some of our facilities are a little older, but I resent your high-handed attitude. Now, I would appreciate it if you left me to get on with the business of running my school and go and sort out your own classes.'

'Very well. But I shall certainly be contacting the County office today. I simply cannot work in these conditions and if necessary, I will resign immediately.'

'You have a contract, Miss Hodges, may I remind you. You can't afford to resign. And as for contacting County Hall, that is my prerogative and not yours. I will do it when and if I see it as necessary. Really, if this is what today's colleges are turning out and calling teaching staff.'

'My college led me to expect decent working conditions for such an important subject, not a mice infested, archaic room with less than the most basic equipment I have ever experienced. Oh and there's evidence of ants and cockroaches too.'

She turned and left his office before the tears she felt ready to burst from her eyes spoilt the effect. Sniffing gently, she went into the staff room and slumped down in a chair. Several people were clapping silently. She stared in surprise. How did anyone know what had happened?

'You spoke quite loudly, love. We all heard what you said through the walls. They are paper thin at this end.' Gary was pouring her a cup of tea and handed it to her, stirring it gently as he did so. She took it gratefully.

'What's going on?' asked Ian coming into the room.

'Our new lady has just given the Old Man a piece of her mind. Seems she's prepared to resign rather than work anywhere near you.' Ian stared at his colleague.

'What on earth have I done wrong?' He looked devastated until he caught Gary's grin twitching at the corners of his mouth. 'OK. You got me. What is it, Lucy? Really, I mean?'

'Just the horrible, filthy room. I can't work like that and it's not fair to expect the kids to clean it up. Whatever he says, I'm here to teach cookery and nutrition and though cleaning up is part of it, a major spring clean certainly isn't.'

'Fair enough. So what's he going to do?'

'Nothing. He has a school to run and I'm only a probationer and clearly an insignificant part of it.'

'Do you have an advisor you can speak to? They can usually pull a few strings.'

'I'm told that's his job not mine.'

'Rubbish,' Ian told her. 'You can just phone her and tell her your complaints. The advisory service is subject based and nothing to do with the Old Man.'

'I'm only on my second day. I can't really afford to get even more high handed. Besides, the only phone's in the secretary's office and I've just blown it with her too.'

'Find the number and demand to use the phone. I'll come with you and distract our Miss Williams.'

'Thanks, but I think I'll have to leave

it today. The number's at home and I don't really see myself standing there looking it up in front of everyone. The Head might come out at any minute and stop me.'

'You stood your ground with him before. Marion will have the number anyhow. Don't be intimidated. It's a foul room. In fact, I'm seriously wondering if I face a health hazard in coming to have a coffee over there.'

Lucy grinned back feebly. She looked pale and her headache was getting worse. This was going to be a day from hell, she could see it coming. Her morning group were fourth years, and from snippets she'd picked up, they were a class to be reckoned with. There was also Marion to meet to discuss syllabus and plans for the term.

It was a dull day, starting to rain. The room looked even more depressing and all the lights had to be put on, just to see across it. There was a knock at the door and a middle aged woman came in.

'Hello, love. I'm Marion Fawcett. I'm the other Home Economist. You're Lucy, aren't you? Oh dear, this looks even worse than I remembered. It hasn't been used since Miss Jenkins left. I always intended to come and give it a bit of a clean, but there was never enough time. I did think the school cleaners might have come in during the summer, though. Maybe you should have a word with the Head.'

'I've already had several words. I wanted to phone the advisor but he says that's his job.'

'Nonsense. You just do it. She's a reasonable woman, our advisor and I know she's been worried about the state of things over here. We've been unable to replace Miss Jenkins all this time, so it's been left for almost a year now.'

'Till Muggins here came along. Thanks, Marion. I will contact her. Now, I suppose I'd better go and collect my class. Though what we're going to do today, I'm at a loss to know. Seems ironic to do basic hygiene in these surroundings.'

'Do some meal planning and promise them they will be able to make their own lunch in a week or two. That will get them really excited and give you a chance to talk about nutrition. You can have some of my recipe books and there are lots of old magazines with foody pictures in. They can make scrap books and cut out recipes.

'Thanks so much. Great idea. And who knows, it might get them actually on my side and I could even get them to make a start on cleaning cookers.'

'OK. I'll send some books over and see you at break. My turn today.'

When break came round it was pouring with rain and the pupils couldn't go out. There was no cosy chat with the other two teachers, as she had to stay and supervise them.

'Here, Miss. Can we go and sort out the back room? Then we could, like have it as a sitting-room and make a den there.'

'Well, we can see if there's anything we can do. It might be a good idea but I warn you, it's an awful mess and it smells horribly damp.'

At this point one of the boys arrived at the door carrying a paper bag.

'Please Miss, Mr Bailey sent this in for you.'

'Thank you. And please thank him too, will you?'

She opened the bag and inside was a fruit pie with a large dollop of cream on top. It looked delicious and she smiled, not liking to eat it in front of her group of girls.

'He's lovely, isn't he? Mr Bailey. We all fancy him, Miss. Do you like him?'

Lucy blushed. She assumed she was near enough to their ages for them to speak to her this way, but it was quite unprofessional of her to acknowledge this.

'I hardly know him. But I'm sure he's an excellent teacher.'

'Wasn't his teaching we were thinking of,' one of them muttered. She pretended not to hear.

By the end of the morning, she was relieved that it hadn't been as dreadful as she had feared. Marion had been right. The idea of cooking their own meal had appealed to them and they were quite excited at the prospect. It would be at least another week however, if this room was to be used for any practical work even if she had got it thoroughly cleaned by then.

Ian arrived as the pupils left. She thanked him for the pie and said she had kept it for lunch.

'Come over to Marion's room. It's warmer in there and much more cheerful.'

She followed him across the little playground and could scarcely believe the difference in the two rooms. A cheerful blaze was going in the ancient solid fuel cooker and the whole room was larger, lighter and airy.

'Wow, this is more like what I was expecting. It's lovely, isn't it?'

'Not bad. But I've been working on it

for many years. There's still some things wrong.'

'It's a palace compared to my room.'

'Right,' Ian announced after they had finished their sandwiches. 'We're going over to the office and you are going to get that advisor of yours on the phone.' Lucy opened her mouth to protest. 'Come on. I'm not letting you suffer any longer than necessary.'

Miss Williams, the secretary, was at lunch so the office was left empty. Ian put his ear to the Head's door.

'It's all right. He's out too. You got the number?' Lucy nodded and picked up the phone, trembling slightly. It all seemed a bit cloak and dagger, as Ian stood at the door to keep watch.

She dialled the number and asked to speak to the Home Economics advisor. She poured out her problems and immediately, the advisor agreed to come over to look around the following morning.

'You'll inform the Head, won't you?'

'Well, yes,' Lucy replied doubtfully.

'More problems there?'

'Well, he won't appreciate me phoning you without telling him.'

'Leave it with me. I'll give him a call this afternoon and tell him I'm making my first probationary visit. No problem.'

Lucy almost wept with relief. Ian came over as she put the phone down and put an arm on her shoulder.

'Well done. I said it would be all right. Now, let's get out of here before we're rumbled.' Lucy grinned with her co-conspirator and rather liking the feel of his arm, went out into the corridor. They got back to the staff room before anyone noticed. 'I should tell you, using the school phone without permission is a punishable offence. If you agree to come out for a drink with me one evening, I promise not to tell anyone.'

'Blackmail, eh? Well, if that's what it takes, thank you. I'd love to.'

'Tomorrow? Celebrate the visit from on high and the satisfactory conclusion to our lunch time's work.'

'Thanks. That would be great. But I'll have to check on train times.'

'I'll drive over to Laston. Not far and I'm sure there's somewhere there to have a drink. What do you say?'

'Thanks again. I'll look forward to it.'

Things were certainly looking up all round. Ian Bailey was certainly someone whose company she would enjoy outside school as well as during the days.

When she got home that evening, a strange car was parked outside their home.

'Hello, Lucy. I got tired of waiting for your call,' Joe announced, as he climbed out of the car.

'What are you doing here? And whose is the car?'

4

'I came to see you, of course,' Joe said with a grin. 'And this is my company car. I had to be in the area so thought I'd drop in to see you and maybe meet your mum?'

'Well, yes of course. Come in.' Lucy was trembling slightly and took a deep breath to try and calm herself down. In some ways, seeing Joe was the last thing she would have chosen. After her awful day and argument with the Head, she wanted to curl up with a nice hot drink and pour out her woes to her understanding mother. Besides, she knew she looked a mess and felt grubby after her day at school. 'Hi, Mum, I'm home. And we have a visitor,' she called out. Sylvia came through wiping her hands on a kitchen towel.

'Hello, love. Oh, hello. Do I know you?' she said smiling at Joe.

'I'm Anne's brother. I dropped Lucy off after the wedding and as I was passing, thought I'd call in. Hope you don't mind.' He held out his hand to shake hers.

'Of course not. I'll put the kettle on, shall I? Tea all right for you?'

'That would be wonderful. Thank you. If it's not too much trouble, of course.' He smiled at her and she was instantly won over. She set great store by good manners and Joe certainly displayed them by the ton.

'Do sit down. Make yourself at home.' He sat on the large comfy sofa and looked quite at home. He'd even managed to avoid the loose spring, Lucy noticed. She excused herself and went into the small kitchen.

'Sorry, Mum. He was waiting outside and I could hardly turn him away.'

'That's all right, love. I can't really ask him to stay for supper though. It's chops and I only got two. I suppose he could have mine and I could always do myself an egg.'

'Don't be silly. I doubt he'll stay long in any case. I've got some stuff to do this evening. I'd better get back to him.' Their conversation had been conducted in whispers and she knew he'd realise they'd been discussing him. He smiled again as she went back into the room.

'Sorry. Perhaps I shouldn't have dropped by so unexpectedly. Would you prefer me to leave?'

'No, it's fine. Stay for a cup of tea anyhow, but I do have some work to do tonight. How's Anne getting on? Have you spoken to her?'

'Not since she started work. How's it going with you?'

Once she started on the subject, Lucy poured out her troubles and even let some of her anger show. She stopped talking and laughed.

'Gosh, I bet you wish you'd never asked. Anyway, I'm seeing the Advisor tomorrow so hope she will be able to do something to help. So, who have you been seeing today?'

'Just a client. I shall probably be

working in Hanley for a few weeks. I'd like to think we might see something of each other while I'm here. If you'd like to, of course.'

'Well,' she began doubtfully, 'I'm flattered of course, but I have a lot of work ahead of me and my time will be rather filled. Besides, you're so much older than me.' She was trying to be polite. His reputation had often been a subject of conversation between her and her friend, Anne, and she certainly didn't want to be just another in his string of girlfriends.

'At least come out for a drink one evening. Or a meal.'

'It's not a good idea,' Lucy said feebly.

'For goodness sake. This is the swinging Sixties. You should let your hair down and stop being so serious. Come on, Lucy, enjoy yourself. Let's go to Trentham Gardens Ballroom on Saturday. There's a good band on and it'll be fun. What do you say?'

She was spared from answering as

her mother came in with a tray of tea. Joe leapt to his feet and relieved her of her burden, setting it down on the side table. There was a plate of homemade cakes and the best china had been set out.

'This looks wonderful,' Joe said with a smile at Sylvia. 'Thank you so much, Mrs Hodges.'

'You'd better call me Sylvia.'

'Thank you, Sylvia. I do appreciate this. I'm living in a flat on my own and homemade cakes are a very rare treat.'

They drank tea and chatted comfortably for almost an hour. She decided to invite him to stay for supper after all but much to Lucy's relief, he declined, saying he needed to get back to his own flat before dark. His car lights were a little suspect and he didn't want to get in trouble with his bosses if he wrecked it or got stopped by the police.

'It's kind of you to ask though,' he told Sylvia. 'I was trying to persuade Lucy to come to the dance at Trentham on Saturday. She shouldn't be working herself so hard.'

'That would be nice, wouldn't it, dear?' Lucy glared and Sylvia said no more. There was a brief pause before Joe got up and excused himself.

'I'll call round on Saturday evening, about seven-thirty,' he announced. 'If you decide not to come with me then I shall have to grin and bear it, won't I? But if you do decide to come, then you'll make me very happy. Remember what I said. You need to get out and enjoy yourself. Thanks very much for the tea and cakes and for a nice chat,' he said to Sylvia. 'Lovely to meet you.'

As he drove away, Sylvia stared at her daughter. She simply could not understand why her daughter was so reticent about seeing this well-mannered young man. He was good looking and even had his own car to ferry her around. But wisely, she said nothing about his invitation. Let Lucy sort out her own mind, but if she had been in her daughter's shoes, she was sure she would have snapped up his offer.

Lucy reluctantly unpacked her school things and sighed as she looked at her list of things to bring up with the County Advisor the next morning. As she was leaving, the secretary had told her that a call had been received from County Hall suggesting Miss Palmer would be calling the following day. Lucy feigned surprise and said she would look forward to the visit.

Miss Williams said that the Head would try to bring her over after he had held a meeting with her and that there may be time for Lucy to bring up anything she wanted to. It wasn't quite what she had been hoping for but with any luck, she and Miss Palmer would get some time alone. She had seemed pleasant enough when Lucy had been interviewed. Just in case she did not get time alone however, she had prepared a list of grievances to hand to the advisor should it be necessary.

'So you see, Mum, it's all looking very tenuous. I may not even get the chance to speak to Miss Palmer if the Head has his way. I don't under-stand why he's so against it all.'

'Maybe he feels guilty about the state things have reached. It probably does reflect badly on him in the long run. But I'm proud of you, darling. Standing up to him couldn't have been easy. Especially when you're so new in the school. Now, do you want anything else to eat?'

'I'm fine, thanks. That was lovely. I suppose I'd better look over my endless lists again. And decide how best to put Joe off coming on Saturday.'

'I'd go if I were you. Enjoy yourself for once. What else might you be doing?'

'I'll see. I'll give you a hand with the washing up.'

'Nonsense. Finish off your work and then we'll watch something on televi-sion. There's a panel game I rather wanted to see.'

Lucy arrived at school early the next day and went straight into her horrible room. She'd wondered about asking the caretaker for the stove to be lit, but decided it might make the place look slightly more cheerful. She wanted it to be seen at its worst to make her point. She switched on the ancient water heater and struggled to light the pilot in the other. The small amount of cleaning she had been able to organise made the tables look better, but the old huge cupboard still contained mouse droppings and ants by the score. Unsure of what was going to happen, she prepared some work sheets for the girls who were coming in first lesson and went over to the main school building.

'Oh, Miss Hodges. I trust you got my message about the County Advisor's visit today? I'm very surprised she could spare the time. You're a lucky girl to get such attention. I'll bring her over once we've had our meeting, if she has enough time.'

'Thank you,' Lucy replied meekly. She had every intention of collaring Miss Palmer to herself for as long as she possibly could. 'Do you know when she plans to arrive?'

'Not sure. It will only be a fleeting visit, I expect. I'll offer her lunch, of course, but doubt she'll take it up.'

Lucy forced a smile and continued into the staff room. There were encouraging smiles from several members of staff who knew the situation. Ian came over and put a hand on her shoulder.

'All set?' he asked.

'I guess so. But the Head is taking a personal interest and implies Miss Palmer may not have time to visit my room. I do think she will though. And hopefully, she'll make an excuse to ditch him.'

The morning progressed and coffee time arrived with still no visit. Marion and Ian came to her room so they could leave quickly if necessary.

'Don't worry,' Marion said. 'Miss Palmer is a shrewd old thing. She'll suss out things and make sure she speaks to you alone. Let her know what you're thinking and I'm sure she'll support you. Speaking of which, I can see them coming down the path. Come on, Ian. Let's make ourselves scarce.'

There were a few awkward moments when the Head was hovering around, anxious to hear everything that was being said.

'Doesn't look too bad, does it, Miss Palmer?' he said waving his arms around the dreary room. 'Well, it's certainly not the nicest of my departments. I'd forgotten what a dark room this is. Put some more lights on, Miss Hodges. Shouldn't have the girls working in the gloom. Bad for eyesight.'

'All the lights are on, Sir. And it isn't even a dark day outside. Excuse me. I need to get my class inside now break is over.' She went to the door and organised her class into a line. They filed in quietly and sat at the tables and continued their work. She had warned them of visitors and that she would have to leave them to get on and fortunately, they had all co-operated. Miss Palmer smiled approvingly and chatted about the work they had been set.

'Excellent, Miss Hodges. I thoroughly approve of that. Now, don't let me keep you, Mr Grissom, we have a few specific matters to discuss.'

'But I have set the morning aside for you. Shouldn't we talk in my office? I have organised lunch if you have time.'

'Actually, no thank you. I have brought a packed lunch and hoped Lucy and I could continue our meeting over lunchtime and maybe I can see Marion at the same time.' Lucy beamed. This was just what she'd hoped for. 'So, you can safely leave us to it now. Thank you for your time and for the coffee. I may call in before I leave, but in any case, I'll be in touch soon.' There was nothing for it but that he should leave. He looked furious as he shut the door and stamped off along the driveway. 'Now Lucy, tell me the problems.'

'Maybe I could show you. Sorry it's so cold in here but evidently, we don't have the stove lit until after half term.'

'Nonsense. It's part of your equipment. You need the solid fuel cooker for the girls to have experience using it.' She took out a notepad and began to write. They walked round the room looking at the various problems. She tutted and sighed and continued to write on her pad. When they reached the store rooms at the back, she gasped in horror. 'This rubbish must go. Clear the lot out.'

'But I gather much of it is being stored for use for various functions. There's a load of drama stuff in there.'

'If you choose to assist in school activities, which I'm sure you will, then that's fine. But your classroom is not a dumping ground.' She made further notes. 'There is an enormous amount of work needed here. What I suggest is that you organise some theory lessons in the main school building and use the other room when Marion is having her days off. I'll send our team from County Hall. We'll get the room painted and cleared and order some new equipment. I'll get the cookers changed too. They are due in a few months anyhow so we'll bring that forward. Pity I can't do more, but I'll see that you get the basics organised and that everywhere is cleaned. Does that satisfy you?'

'Oh, Miss Palmer, thank you. Thank you so much. It means a lot to me.'

'Well, it isn't going to be easy for you for the next few weeks but we shall get there. You're very down on basics too. Even simple baking tins are way past being usable. Make a list of the equipment you need and I'll see what we can manage. Our budget is never very much, I'm afraid, so don't be too extravagant in your demands.'

By the time she was leaving, Miss Palmer had brought the first proper smile to Lucy's face since she had walked into the school. She went across to see the Head again and told him of the plans. At the end of the day, he spoke to Lucy again as she left her keys in the office.

'You're a very lucky girl,' he told her patronisingly. 'We've tried to get the rooms improved many times but you obviously said the right things. It's going to be a lot of disruption while the work is done so I shall expect you to co-operate.'

Ian and Marion were delighted.

'Well done. Just shows a bit of nagging in the right place and result. I think we should have that drink to celebrate. What do you say?'

'Thanks. Yes, I'd like that.'

'I'm afraid I can't join you,' Marion said with a glum expression. Lucy smiled at her face. Then the older woman grinned. 'Only teasing. I realise I wasn't actually being invited.'

'Pick you up around seven?'

'Great. Thank you.'

'So, where do you live?' She drew him a little map and gave him a load of directions, too. 'Don't worry. I'm pretty good at finding my way around. See you later.'

She went home feeling happy, excited

and greatly relieved. She did feel slightly guilty about leaving her mother alone for the evening, but she knew Sylvia wouldn't really mind. As it happened, Sylvia had made plans to go out herself.

'They're trying to put together a gardening club and I said I'd go along to discuss how it might work. Didn't think you'd mind being left on your own, but now I don't even need to think about it. Do I get to meet this one?'

'This one? You make it sound as though I'm running a whole string of men. If he arrives before you leave, of course you can meet him.'

As it happened, her mother left before Ian arrived so she didn't meet him after all. They went to a pub in the next village and spent a pleasant evening chatting and discovering things about each other that they would never have time to talk about in the busy school day.

Sylvia had still not returned when

they got back. Lucy made coffee for Ian before he drove away. He gave her a friendly peck on the cheek as he left and she waved him off. He was nice, she thought. Very nice. He seemed open and honest and unpretentious. He was good to look at too, she smiled to herself. Suddenly feeling exhausted, she went up to bed and fell asleep not even knowing whether her mother had returned.

There was a letter on the staff room table when she arrived the next day. She opened it and frowned. It was from the Head and contained a list of rooms she was to use for her lessons and a note stating that as she was now to be based in the main building, she was expected to take over a form of her own. The Senior Mistress would be relieved of her own group so she could use the time for administration purposes. Lucy showed the letter to Ian, who also frowned.

'That's so unfair. He's just making use of you. Getting back at you for getting County involved without his say so.'

'But I don't see why. It's in his interest to make things better, isn't it?'

'Of course. But he likes to feel he's in control of everything and driving it all. Just you wait. He'll be taking all the credit for any improvements. Mark my words, you'll see. Anyhow, thanks again for last night. I enjoyed it.'

'I should be thanking you. You didn't even let me buy you a drink last night.'

'I should think not. You have to wait ages yet before you get any pay. I remember what it's like working in arrears. Don't worry too much about being the form mistress. It's Dorothy's group and they're not a bad lot. Just takes up so much extra time.'

'How do I cope when I have to go across the road on the other days?'

'Maybe Dorothy will take pity on you.'

'Something will have to be done. I can't get in any earlier as there isn't another train I can catch.'

It was soon the weekend and problem of Joe's invitation for Saturday evening.

'What are you going to do, love?' asked Sylvia.

'I don't know. I suppose I haven't got anything else arranged. I'm just not sure about him. I really enjoyed my evening with Ian and wouldn't hesitate if it was him asking me. Funny really. Joe must be about twenty-seven or eight and I don't suppose Ian's that much younger, but it seems sort of right and wrong with Joe.'

'You must do what you think is best. Twenty-seven or eight is hardly Methuselah. Perhaps it's because Ian works in education and Joe in the commercial world.'

'Maybe. What shall I do about the dance though?'

'I'd go. Enjoy yourself. After the week you've had, you could do with a change. You can wear that nice green dress with the full skirt. You look lovely in that.'

'OK. But I shan't see him again after this.'

'You don't know that. You might enjoy it.'

'He is a pretty good dancer actually.'

'Well, there you are then.'

By seven-thirty, Lucy was ready and waiting. Maybe he wouldn't turn up and she'd be spared all her worries. She saw his car stopping outside and called goodbye to her mother. Sylvia came to the door and immediately, Joe got out of the car and came over to shake her hand.

'I'll take good care of her,' he said cheerily. 'I'm so pleased she decided to come.'

'Excuse me. I'm here. Me. Lucy.'

'Sorry, love. I just wanted to reassure your mother. We won't be too late back. Soon after midnight, when it ends. Come on then, Luce ... let's get rocking.'

5

It was a good evening and to her surprise, Lucy enjoyed it all very much. Joe was courteous and attentive and as she had remarked to her mother, an excellent dancer. He spun her round in several complex rock and roll turns and some of the other dancers stood back to watch them. Flushed and laughing at the end of the number, they bowed to the spontaneous applause.

'Wow, I need at least a gallon of lemonade,' Lucy gasped. 'I never knew I could do all that.'

'You're very good. Followed my lead like a dream. It was fun. Wouldn't you like something stronger than lemonade?'

'No thanks. That's fine.'

He held her close for the last waltz and she quite enjoyed the sensation of moving so completely in harmony.

When he tried to kiss her though, it was a different matter. She tried to push him away, but he was persistent and rather too strong for her to succeed. He was kissing very thoroughly and holding her much too tightly in the middle of the dance floor. When she finally managed to escape, she spoke to him angrily.

'Couldn't you see that I didn't want you to kiss me like that?'

'Come on, Lucy. Grow up. You've been coming on to me all evening. What was I supposed to think?'

'I wasn't. I didn't. I was just enjoying the dancing. It certainly wasn't an invitation for you to ... to ... well nothing. I'm sorry if you got the wrong end of the stick. I'd like to go home now please. Straight home.'

He looked at her furiously and went to the cloakroom, handing over the ticket for her coat. Without saying a word, he helped her into it and led the way outside to the car park. Polite as ever he opened the door and assisted

78

her in. They drove back in silence and he pulled up outside.

'Thank you, Joe. I did enjoy myself, truly. I'm sorry if I didn't live up to your expectations.'

'My mistake. I thought you were more mature, but one can always get the wrong impression.'

'Do you want to come in for coffee?'

'No thanks. There's not much point is there? I'm disappointed in you. Anne said you were such fun, but I guess she's only your age as well. Different interpretation of fun. See you.'

'Yes. Bye and thanks again.' He raised a hand as he drove away at rather too fast a speed for the narrow lane. 'I suppose that's that,' she muttered as she went inside.

Luckily, her mother was already in bed so she didn't need to make any explanations or even discuss the evening till the next morning. At least it gave her time to collect her thoughts and come to terms with it all.

Of course she had been kissed before.

She and Alistair had spent a lot of time kissing but somehow, it was different. Clearly, Joe was not the right man for her from the start. It had taken time for her to know that Alistair was not Mr Right but they were more or less the same age and probably experience. Interesting.

She began to think about Ian again. She wondered why he hadn't asked her out over the weekend. Obviously, he had something to occupy him. Could he possibly qualify as a Mr Right? She felt a frisson of excitement as she thought more about him. Too early to say but he certainly seemed a very attractive companion and who could tell what the future might hold?

As the term progressed, the modernisation of her room was taking shape. She had been impressed at first at the speed Miss Palmer had moved to get the workmen in. Exciting packages of equipment had arrived and there was a large van parked outside for several days, to take away a lot of the rubbish from the store rooms.

She went out with Ian about once a week and to her relief, had heard nothing more from Joe. She still felt frustrated that she wasn't teaching in the way she had hoped for, but she was putting in some basic knowledge in hygiene and nutrition.

At last, the work was finished and she could move back into her room. Even the Head came over to look at what had been done.

'Excellent. I'm so pleased I thought of getting County Hall involved,' he announced. 'Leaves you free to become more involved with the rest of the school. Now, we have a Governor's meeting next Thursday. I need you to provide us with afternoon tea. Sandwiches, cake. You know the sort of thing. It's usually served in the old library. Get a couple of girls to assist you with serving it. Around three-thirty is usual.'

'But . . . ' she began. What was the point? She had been warned that he would take any credit for anything that was done to her room. The Governor's meeting however, was a different matter.

'The Governor's meeting,' she said. 'Are you suggesting I have to get some pupils to stay on after school and that you also expect me to work on after school hours?'

'You're the cookery teacher. It's expected. No problems are there? Good.' He turned and went out of the room.

Lucy felt her temper rising. The cookery teacher indeed. It was as if he thought she was there just to provide a service when he wanted. Who had been providing these teas after Miss Jenkins had left? She doubted Marion would have done it. Not that she disliked her colleague, but she was getting the impression that she did the barest minimum possible and certainly nothing that involved after hours working. She was in her probationary year and if the Head did not give his approval at the end of it, she would fail as a teacher.

'Talk about blackmail,' she muttered

to Ian when break came.

'Never mind. I usually get to mend all the desks and chairs if they get damaged. We're the unpaid maintenance and support team. Tell you what, I stay on late on Thursdays to run my evening class. Why don't we have something to eat after your duties. I could collect fish and chips or something and we can eat it in your palatial new premises.'

'That sounds nice. Not sure about the palatial though.'

After he had gone back to his own room, she thought about their relationship, if such it could be called. It never seemed to progress further than a casual peck on the cheek as she left him. They talked about their work for much of the time they were together. Her mum thought he was lovely and had really taken to him on the couple of occasions he had come in for coffee. She'd even suggested inviting him for a meal at the weekend a couple of times, but he had always refused.

He was slightly cagey about talking about personal things, though Lucy was certain he was not committed to anyone in any way. It seemed strange. He clearly enjoyed her company and they had an easy, comfortable friendship. Perhaps he simply didn't want any serious entanglements.

After the meeting, where she had politely served tea to the rather odd collection of people who comprised the Governor's meeting, she took the dirty crockery back to her room and began to wash up. The two fourth year girls who had helped prepare everything had gone home. The evenings were drawing in and she didn't want them to go home in the dark. Ian arrived a few minutes later, clutching two newspaper wrapped packets.

'Are we having plates or shall we eat it out of the paper?'

'I vote for paper,' Lucy said drying her hands. 'No washing up.'

'Fingers then, I gather.'

'Absolutely. I've got extra salt and

vinegar in the cupboard. Nobody ever puts enough on for me. Besides, chip shops always dilute the vinegar to make it go further.'

'Really? I never knew that. I got mushy peas too. Hope you like them.'

'Wow, you really know how to treat a girl, don't you? May need a fork after all.'

They ate the savoury meal and licked sticky fingers at the end, giggling as they did so. Lucy reached over to wipe away a dribble of mushy peas from his chin. He took her hand and pulled her towards him. Then he kissed her. Properly, on the lips. She felt herself melting towards him and then felt the stool slipping away. In a burst of giggle, she almost landed on the floor but he grabbed her and dragged her on to his knee.

'Sorry, Ian. I quite spoiled a romantic moment.' He was about to reply when his jaw fell as the door opened.

'Exactly what is going on here?' the Head demanded. 'How dare you use school facilities for your . . . your personal goings on. It is also totally inappropriate for two of my staff members to be seen consorting together.' Lucy almost laughed out loud. Consorting together? That was rich. Very quaint. 'I need your assurances that nothing like this will happen again. Abusing school premises this way. What are you doing here in any case?'

'I was clearing up after your meeting. Ian, Mr Bailey, is taking an evening class and we decided to share supper.'

'It was hardly sharing supper I witnessed. Suppose one of the governors had been with me? They might have wanted to see the improvements in this room that I have organised for you. I begin to wonder why I bothered if this is the sort of misuse you intended. What would it have looked like if they had walked in on two of my staff behaving so inappropriately? Do I have your guarantee this that relationship will cease immediately?'

'I'm sorry, Sir,' Ian said politely, 'but

we are friends and will remain so. There is nothing to indicate that we shouldn't see each other outside school if we choose to.'

'Not good. Not good at all. You've hardly made an auspicious start to your teaching career, Miss Hodges. I should think carefully about your future. I should remind you that you are still on probation.' Angrily, he turned and left the room. They looked at each other and were about to burst into laughter when the Head returned. 'Make sure you lock the doors and return the keys to my office.'

'I have to finish clearing up. I trust you will still be there for another half-an-hour?' Lucy asked innocently.

'Hmm. You may take the keys home on this occasion. Unless you leave the clearing till the morning and get the girls to do it.'

'Oh, I couldn't do that. I have pre-pared a syllabus to follow and I hadn't incorporated Governor's teas into the scheme.' Her innocent expression made the Head frown again.

Ian looked as if he was about to explode with laughter.

'Go girl,' he said cheerfully as the Head left. 'I think he met his match.'

'Nonsense. I'm screwing up all chances of getting his approval for my probationary year. But I do resent him taking all the credit for this room, after all my efforts.'

'I'm sorry, anyway.'

'Sorry for what? Kissing me?'

'I shouldn't have done it. Especially not here, with all the lights on. I bet that's why he came in. He could see us through the windows.'

'Maybe. Actually Ian, I'm not sorry you kissed me. I enjoyed it.' He did not respond and looked rather awkward.

'I'd better go and get ready for my class.'

'Yes, of course. Thanks again for the fish and chips.' She finished tidying up, locked the doors and left to catch her train home.

She felt puzzled. What was Ian

hiding? Perhaps he did have a girlfriend and did merely want to be friends with Lucy. If that was the case, why didn't he say so? He really didn't seem the sort who would two-time anyone. She acknowledged that she would like them to become more than friends but on his current behaviour, that seemed some-what unlikely.

'How did it go, love?' Sylvia asked when her daughter finally arrived home.

'Mixed,' came the reply and she recounted her day, omitting the kiss incident. She wondered how things would seem the following day when they met again. There was no chance to speak until break and that was inter-rupted by the girls who were fussing over their cookery. Officially, they were supposed to play outside during breaks, but as the new room was unfamiliar to them, they wanted to check on the ovens every five minutes, it seemed.

'We'll maybe catch up at lunch time,' Ian said finally.

When lunchtime arrived, she felt distinctly nervous for some reason. She was expecting some sort of explanation from him and sensed that she wasn't going to like it.

'I wondered if you'd like to go out dancing one evening. Well, on Saturday, actually. If you have nothing better to do. And if you're free of course.'

'Gosh. Yes, I'd love to. Sorry, that was a bit unexpected. I thought you were about to confess to a wife and family or at least a girlfriend hidden away.'

'No, nothing like that. But I do have commitment of a sort. I was thinking about the Head's comments last night. I think I felt a bit uneasy about him catching us in a, well compromising position in his eyes. But his suggestions about us not meeting outside school was quite preposterous. He has no right whatever to dictate to us on such things. As long as we remain professional in school, I don't see anything wrong in our meeting. So, how does Trentham sound?'

'Great,' she said happily. 'I love dancing and theirs is the best ballroom in the district.' She remembered her last visit there with a tremor of discomfort. This time it would be great, with a man she really liked.

She wore her favourite green dress again, as Ian had never seen it before. The room was crowded and the music loud, so there was little opportunity to talk. Ian was a surprisingly good dancer and they rarely missed a dance. At last, she was gasping and they went into the bar for a drink.

'You're quite a mover,' she laughed. 'I've never managed to do the cha-cha-cha quite so expertly.'

'My mother was a ballroom dance teacher at one time, so I got dragged along to her classes from an early age. Once I was tall enough, I was the most popular partner in the room. Always lots more women than men at these things. Do you know that chap over there?' he asked suddenly. 'Only he's been staring at you for the past five minutes.'

She turned and to her horror, she saw Joe standing at the bar. He raised his glass to her and came over. A girl trailed after him.

'Lucy, darling. How lovely to see you again. You're looking good. I always did love you in that dress. I remember it well. Oh, this is Melanie, by the way. Aren't you going to introduce me to your latest conquest?'

Ian was looking distinctly uncomfortable.

'This is Ian. A friend and colleague of mine. Ian, this is Joe, the brother of one of my college friends.'

'Oh come on, darling. We were once much more than that. Don't try to belittle what we once meant to each other.'

'For goodness sake, Joe. We had one date. One disaster.'

'Not quite how I remember it. But, if that's the way you want to play it.' He gave a knowing wink to Ian. 'These girls, eh? Swinging sixties personified. Nice to meet you again, Lucy and I hope this one gives you everything you always wanted. Ciao.' He turned and steered the poor Melanie back into the ballroom.

'How dare he?' Lucy burst out. 'What conceit. He was lying, Ian. Truly.'

'If you say so.' His voice sounded cold and the closeness had all evaporated. 'Do you want to dance some more?'

'Sure. But I beg you, don't take any notice of his insinuations. We really did have only one date and when I wouldn't go along with what he wanted, we parted on bad terms.'

'I'm really not interested. Now, let's dance, or would you prefer to go home now?'

They danced some more, but the fun had quite disappeared. Any progress she had thought she and Ian might be making, had also disappeared after Joe's horrid insinuations. After a short while, she suggested they might leave.

Ian said little as they drove home and

he was clearly upset. She began to feel irritated. Surely he couldn't believe that she had never been out with anyone all the time she was away at college? She was almost twenty-two and . . . well, one of her old school friends was expecting her second child so she could hardly consider herself a child. As they stopped outside her mother's cottage, she invited him in for a coffee.

'Better get back,' he said politely. 'Busy day ahead of me tomorrow.'

'Ian, can I ask you something?' He nodded. 'Are you upset about Joe? I mean, up till then, you were enjoying the evening and well, you seemed really warm and friendly. Then you went all cold on me.'

'I'm sorry. I didn't much like the way he was pawing you. Seemed to know you very well and I suppose I was just disappointed. I'd thought you were different from other girls. But I should have known someone like you was bound to be a bit of a swinger, just as your Joe suggested.'

'He's not or ever has been my Joe. Oh for heaven's sakes. He was right. This is the sixties, but you needn't think that means I don't behave with a sense of decency. But, if that's how you feel, there's nothing I can do about it. Thanks for taking me out. I did enjoy most of the evening. Goodnight. See you on Monday.'

'Goodnight, Lucy. Enjoy your week-end. Dare say you'll have plenty to keep you busy tomorrow.'

There was no kiss, not even a peck on the cheek. He shut the door behind her and drove away. She went into the house and her mother appeared in her dressing-gown peering round the door to make sure her daughter was alone. She put some milk to heat while Lucy told her about the ruined evening.

'It was awful, Mum. You'd think Joe and I were practically engaged the way he talked. I even felt sorry for the girl he was with.'

'What was that song? *Que sera, sera.* If things are meant to happen they will.

I'm sorry though, love. I know you were becoming fond of Ian.'

'I was. Am. But what's really awful is that I have to work with him every day.'

6

It was difficult on Monday morning. Ian didn't exactly ignore her, but nor was he his usual friendly, light-hearted self. He even refused coffee at break time, saying he was too busy. She tried not to think about him and got on with her work. Planning lessons and marking theory work kept her busy. She and Marion got on well enough, but the older woman seemed to suffer from ill-health and was never very enthusiastic about her work. Being so far from the main part of school meant that she didn't get to know many of the rest of the staff and without Ian, she did sometimes feel a little lonely.

'Are we making Christmas cakes?' one of the fourth years asked during their lesson.

'Goodness, I suppose we're getting a bit late in the term for that. I hadn't

realised how the weeks had flown by.'
She made some calculations. Amazingly, there only three weeks left before the final week of the Christmas term. 'I'm sorry, but with the renovations to this room and everything, I'm really not sure we have the time. I'd need to send letters home and everything and that just isn't possible in the time we have left. Next year perhaps.'

'But we might not all be here next year. Some of us will be leaving.'

'We'll make something special for Christmas. I'll look up some recipes and we can plan it next week.'

'What sort of somethings?' one asked suspiciously.

'I don't know. Some biscuits or maybe some sweets. Truffles and marzipan fruits.'

'We don't eat truffles in our house,' one girl announced.

'You don't even know what they are,' snapped one of her friends.

'We could make chocolate logs,' suggested Lucy. 'They won't cost as much and can look very festive.'

'Cor, yer,' they replied, almost in unison. Harmony was restored and she began to write out recipes for them. She planned to buy some small decorations for each of them to use and worked out how the cost could be kept down. Many of them came from rather poor backgrounds where every penny counted and she'd hate for any of them to be disappointed because they couldn't afford to join in.

Her own wages were pretty low, but she was sure she could afford to subsidise a few extras. She felt slightly annoyed with herself for being so wrapped up in her own affairs that she hadn't realised how much she needed to organise for the coming festivities. But, now that she had realised it, she would make plans for all her classes to do something special for Christmas.

Lucy felt quite cheerful when she got home that evening. Her mother was going out for the evening so she had the place to herself and spread out papers and books all over the table. She cut out some templates to make little boxes for the younger groups to use for some marzipan sweets and worked out how they might decorate them for gifts for their parents.

Then she worked out how to cut some rectangles of card to be covered to make cake boards and finally, made a shopping list of all the things she needed to buy to complete her plans. Maybe she could get some finance from the school for some of her things. After all, there had to be some sort of budget available but even if there wasn't, she would use a little of her own money. At ten-thirty, her mother was still not back and so Lucy went to bed.

She was slightly curious about these evenings out but her mother had merely muttered something about a gardening club. She was pleased that Sylvia was finding a bit of social life at last. She had looked after her daughter for so long, it was high time she made something of her own life.

As the end of term approached, there seemed to be a number of activities planned and Lucy joined in with jumble sales which she hated and Christmas parties, which she loved. Ian kept himself aloof and she missed him. She glanced at him during one of the children's parties and couldn't help but wish that things had been different. She would have enjoyed going to parties with him or dancing again.

She cursed Joe and his insinuations and wondered whether she could say anything to Ian to make him think better of her. It was so unfair. She wished she could have a chat to her college friend, Anne, and confide in her. She had been so supportive when Lucy and Alistair had ended their relationship. Maybe they could meet up over the holidays and compare notes on their first term as teachers and she might even persuade Anne to tell her brother what a rotten mess he'd made of her life.

The party was drawing to a close and

a whole collection of exhausted looking staff were breathing sighs of relief. Lucy was just wondering if she might make her escape when Ian came over to her and invited her to dance. The pupils were all staggering round the floor in vague attempts at doing the waltz.

'Let's show them how it's done,' Ian said with a grin. He took her in his arms and they sailed round the floor in complete harmony. The pupils stopped their own attempts and stood watching.

'Ready for a turn?' he breathed and swept her round in a series of complicated spins. She followed him perfectly and the youngsters clapped. Flushed and laughing, Lucy wondered if this was an olive branch and allowed herself to dream a little.

'You're very good, you two,' Gary said applauding with the rest. 'You ought to try and teach some of this lot. We should start a dancing club after school. What do you say?'

'I'd be happy to,' Lucy burst out without thinking.

'I'm really rather too busy,' Ian said. 'Maybe sometime in the future we could think about it.' Then he mumbled something about having too many commitments and rushed away. Lucy smiled wanly and shrugged.

'Something going on I don't know about?' asked Gary. He was almost old enough to be her father, she realised and he seemed concerned.

'Nothing at all,' Lucy replied. She felt very miserable and turned away before she was forced to say anything more to her kindly colleague. She helped with the clearing up and suddenly exhausted, said her goodbyes and set off for the station. She saw Ian's car beginning to move from its parking space and she hesitated for a moment and then gave him as cheerful a wave as she could manage. He slowed and wound down the window.

'Do you want a lift to the station?' he began, but was interrupted by a cry from behind them.

'Lucy, Darling.' She swung round

and to her utter amazement, saw Alistair standing beside a shiny new mini. 'How's about this then? I couldn't resist coming to show you. I've missed you so much.' Before she could even protest or say a word, he flung his arms round her and kissed her firmly on the lips. She struggled to push him away but his arms were tightly around her and she was helpless to struggle.

'Ian, I'm sorry. Alistair, get off me. Ian I'd love a lift to the station please.'

'It looks as if you already have a lift. See you.' He drove away rather too quickly and Lucy crumbled.

'Alistair, how could you? Grabbing me like that and kissing me. We're finished, remember?'

'I've been waiting here for over an hour. Whatever time are you teachers supposed to finish these days?'

'It was a Christmas party for the kids. We were late clearing up. Now, if you'll excuse me, I have a train to catch.' She began to walk away but he caught her arm.

'Don't be ridiculous. I'll drive you

home. It's dark and cold. Don't be so prickly and stubborn. You look done in.'

She had to admit, he was right. She felt exhausted, both physically and emotionally. A drive back in a nice warm car or fighting her way on to a crowded train with a long walk down the lane . . . here was no competition. Despite her better judgement she agreed that a lift would be great.

They chatted on the way back and he said that he had a new job in Stafford, hence the car. It was only a few miles away and he thought it would be easy for them to see each other.

'I've really missed you,' he told her. 'I wanted to call before, but I wasn't sure how you'd take it.'

'I'm just accepting a lift back, OK? Nothing more. If I wasn't completely shattered, I wouldn't even be doing that. I don't want to see you any more and there's no future for us.'

'If you say so.'

'How did you know where I worked by the way?'

'Someone told me at the wedding. Can't remember who. I just looked at maps and asked various people where the school was. Easy really.' He stopped the car outside the cottage.

Sylvia opened the door and peered out and then came outside.

'Hello?' she said, surprised to see the strange car. 'Oh, is that Alistair? Goodness me, what a surprise.'

'Yes, Mrs Hodges. Nice to see you again.'

'Nice to see you too. Would you like to come in for a cup of tea?'

Lucy frowned, but she could say nothing. Her mother was welcoming her ex-boyfriend like a long lost friend and she could do nothing about it.

Sylvia bustled around making tea and produced a plate of freshly made mince pies. She seemed nervous, as if she wasn't sure how to behave with this young man. Lucy tried to be casual and politely chatty, but she wished he would go.

'Perhaps you'd like to stay and have

some supper with us? It's only cottage pie but there's plenty and I can easily add a few more vegetables to make it go round.'

'That's really kind of you. Some real home cooking. Sounds amazing. I'm living in a sort of glorified bedsit at the moment, so the best I can manage is a can of beans and toast.' He glanced at Lucy and pretended not to notice her glare. 'Quite like old times, isn't it?' he said cheerfully.

'The only thing is, I'm going out in a little while. Still, that will give you plenty of time to chat.'

'Thanks, Mrs Hodges, but I can't stay long. I have things to do before tomorrow,' Alistair told her.

'Where are you going, Mum?' Lucy asked curiously.

'Oh, just some gardening club thing. I'm sure you won't mind.'

'You're spending an awful lot of time on this gardening club. I hope they're not taking advantage of your kindness.'

'Don't be silly, dear. I'm thoroughly

enjoying myself.' She was blushing slightly and Lucy stared curiously but she said nothing, especially in front of her unwelcome guest. Clearly there was something going on that she was not being told.

They sat down with coffee after her mother had left. Alistair wasted no time.

'Lucy, I love you. I've tried going out with other girls, but they mean nothing to me.'

'Like that one you took to Sarah's wedding?'

'That was a total disaster. But you're the one, Lucy. Just let's spend some time together. You don't know that we won't find each other again. Come out to dinner with me tomorrow evening. Let's talk.' He leaned over to her and took her hand gently and kissed her fingers. Then he put his arms round her and tried to kiss her properly.

'Please. Stop. I don't . . . '

'Come out with me tomorrow and let's talk it through. You're tired now and clearly quite emotional. We'll go somewhere special and well, if we're in public, we have to be civilised at least.' He grinned and stood up. 'Promise me?'

'All right,' she agreed doubtfully. 'But don't hold out any hopes. I mean it. We're over.'

'I'll pick you up here if that's all right. I won't be finishing working quite so early tomorrow. Seven o'clock all right?'

'OK. But . . . ' she began. He put a finger on her lips to stop saying anything more. As he drove away, Lucy's doubts began all over again. Why on earth had she agreed to this dinner date? She went back into the house. She felt totally exhausted and still had a few things to do for the next day. It was the last group she would be teaching before the holidays and she needed to make sure she had everything ready for the chocolate log session.

She found the pack of tiny plastic robins and the little holly leaves and counted them out. She hoped there were enough for each child but for the life of her, couldn't remember how many were in that group. She'd left the class list in her desk. Too bad. Nothing she could do about it now.

She allowed herself to think about Ian. Why did Alistair have to turn up at that very moment, just when Ian was going to take her to the station. It had been the first time he'd been anywhere near her in ages and after that dance at the party, she'd really believed the ice was beginning to melt. Feeling almost near to tears, she went into the kitchen and made some cocoa. She was curled up on the sofa when her mother returned.

'What is it, love? What's wrong?'

'Oh everything. Alistair, mainly. His timing couldn't have been worse.'

'Lucy, I'm sorry,' Sylvia told her, giving her a hug. 'I thought you seemed pleased to see Alistair again. I thought I was doing the right thing asking him to stay for supper.'

'It's all right, Mum. You weren't to know. It was such a shock seeing him again and he seemed to think we were just going to pick up again. But I can't. I don't love him. And stupidly, I agreed to go out to dinner tomorrow to talk things over. I really don't want to go, but I didn't even take his phone number to cancel it.'

'It's your chap at school behind all this, isn't it?'

'I thought we might be able to mend the fences, but just when Ian was offering me a lift to the station, Alistair had to turn up. My reputation will now be shot and Ian will think I'm some sort of man-crazed idiot.'

'And here was me thinking everything was going to be lovely with Alistair again. Full reconciliation and who knows? I must keep my nose out of your affairs and stop making assumptions.'

'I think I *have* fallen in love with Ian and it's all hopeless. He's just not interested, but after today, I had thought we might be friends again. It's horrible working so closely and having him hate me.'

'Come on now, love. I'm sure he doesn't hate you.'

'But he's seen me with two other men and must think I'm just another flirt. Anyway, enough of my troubles. Tell me about your gardening club. There's something more to it, isn't there?'

'Actually, I've been seeing someone. You don't mind do you?'

'Seeing someone? As in going out with someone? That's great, tell me all about him. Where you met and everything.'

'It's Jim. You know, the chap who's been coming to help with the garden. He did ask me to help organise the gardening club and well, it just went on from there. You really don't mind do you?' she asked her daughter anxiously.

'Mum, I'm thrilled. He's a lovely bloke and you deserve some happiness after all these years of working to keep me. It's great. So, how long has it been going on?'

'Only a few weeks really. But we found we got on really well together when we chatted over tea. He's been very kind to me and never takes a penny for the work he does. Says he hasn't got much garden himself and enjoys it so much, he's glad to help me. I didn't want to say anything until I was sure we were really getting more serious.'

They chatted for another half hour until Lucy could stifle her yawns no longer.

'Sorry, Mum. I'm shattered. One more cookery class and then one more day of clearing up the room and Christmas, here I come. Is Jim coming for Christmas Day?'

'I haven't asked him. But would you mind?'

'Course not. I look forward to it. Much more than this date of mine tomorrow.' All the same, as she lay in bed, she wondered if sharing her mother was going to be difficult after all these years. Why on earth had she suggested Christmas of all days? She should have taken time to get to know him a little before inviting him to share such a special day.

7

At the end of the morning, Lucy was thrilled with the results of her class's efforts. Sixteen perfect chocolate logs sat on sixteen silver boards with their proud owners grinning with delight.

'Thanks ever so much, Miss,' one of them said.

'Yer, thanks, Miss,' echoed the rest. Her supply of robins and holly leaves had been exactly right and made all the difference to the Christmassy look.

'They look great. Now, I've got some cellophane to put over them and then perhaps we can ask Mrs Fawcett to come and look at your work before you take them away. Will you each write your name on these labels so we can make certain they don't get mixed up.' She handed out sticky labels, knowing that they could easily get muddled and cause great upset. Once wrapped and labelled, she sent one of the girls over to the next room to invite their visitor. They were delighted to feel so special and Lucy knew she had made some friends in the group.

'That was a lovely thing to do,' Marion told her. 'They'll remember that for the rest of their time in school.'

'I'm planning to organise some meals next term and maybe let them invite their class teachers over.'

'Nice idea, but don't forget costs. There's no money to subsidise anything and you can't afford to be out of pocket yourself.'

'No, you're right. I'll have to work out something. Maybe I should have word with the Head, now things have calmed down a bit. He actually smiled at me the other day.'

Once the school day was nearing an end, Lucy began to feel nervous about the coming evening. She had scarcely seen Ian to try to explain things and he seemed as cool as ever. Perhaps he was just busy, clearing his own room for the holiday. If she really did love him, she would have to get used to the idea that it wasn't ever going to be easy to let him know. How could she love him? She was too young to know such a thing and in any case, she hardly knew him. Not really.

'Go on. Convince yourself,' she muttered out loud as she packed her bag to go home.

Inevitably, the train was late and it started to rain as she walked along the lane home. It was becoming bitterly cold and the rain turned to sleet. She was drenched by the time she arrived at the cottage and felt more like curling up with a hot water bottle than going out for a potentially difficult dinner.

'Do you want a bath?' Sylvia asked when Lucy arrived home. 'Only I'll need to put the water on to heat if you do.'

'It's all right, Mum. I'll just have a wash and dry my hair. It's too cold in our bathroom to strip off. I could do with some hot tea though. It's freezing out here. Maybe Alistair will forget about it and stay at home.'

'I doubt it. He seems pretty keen. He's such a nice boy. I don't understand what you don't like about him. You're clearly going nowhere with this Ian of yours. You and Alistair were close enough for all that time at college.'

'Oh, Mum. I just don't care for him the way I should. Yes, he's nice enough and doubtless has a great future, but I just don't feel the same way about him. He does seem keen, but I really don't feel the same way.'

'Sorry, I'm interfering again, aren't I? I'll go and put the kettle on. At least I can manage that all right.'

Lucy sat in front of the fire, gradually drying out and feeling more comforted. She told Sylvia about her successful morning and the pleasure her class had shown at the end of the lesson. She cheered up and gave her Mum a hug as she went to change.

'Jim was thrilled we asked him for Christmas, by the way.'

'Surely he didn't come to do any gardening today?'

'Much too wet and cold. No, he just came round for a pot of tea and a chat. He had the afternoon off work. They'd finished an order and there was nothing more to do.'

'What does he do?'

'He works at Wedgewood's. Some sort of shift work. That's why he can come and do the gardening at odd times. Anyway, you'd better get yourself ready.'

Lucy went up to her room and reflected on the latest situation with her mother and this man. It felt very strange after all these years after being just the two of them. She really did feel a bit jealous, she acknowledged but she was undoubtedly going to move on herself and wouldn't want to live here forever. If her mother wanted to make a new life for herself, she had every right to do so.

However Lucy was feeling right now, she must never show it. Her mother had always put her first and made endless sacrifices for her only daughter. I am just so selfish, she chided herself and felt ashamed.

She sighed and looked in her wardrobe to find something to wear. She settled for a midi length skirt and simple blouse. She added a lacy cardigan in case the room was chilly. She supposed she should wear something a bit more sparkly as it was nearly Christmas, but she wasn't in the mood.

'You look nice, dear. Are you sure you'll be warm enough?'

'I'll put my thick coat on. I expect the restaurant will be warm, even in this weather. Just listen to that wind. I must be mad to go out in this.'

'I think we'll get a telephone put in. Suppose you couldn't get back? You couldn't even let me know and I'd lie awake all night worrying.'

'Maybe I shouldn't go. Could we afford a telephone? I must say, it would be nice. I could let you know if I was working late or missed the train.'

'I think we might. Now you're working and contributing to the expenses. Be easier for you to cancel unwanted dates too,' she added with a wicked grin.

'Easier for him to pester me to arrange another one.'

'Well, we wouldn't have to tell everyone the number. He need never know. I'll look into it after Christmas.'

'Here's Alistair,' Lucy said as she looked out of the window. 'Wish me luck.'

'Have a nice time and for goodness sake, enjoy yourself. No reason not enjoy a good meal even if the company isn't the one you'd like it to be.'

Alistair had booked a table at one of the large hotels in the nearby town. He was wearing a smart suit and was clearly on his best behaviour. He was attentive and courteous and not in the least bit pushy. Lucy felt very relieved and even began to enjoy herself. The food was perfectly cooked and quite delicious.

'Will you have a dessert?' he asked when the main course was finished.

'I don't think I have room for it.'

'They do a marvellous sweet trolley. Take a look and see if you can't be tempted.'

She turned round and looked at the laden trolley. There certainly was a splendid selection and she wondered if she might just squeeze one of the delicious, calorie laden creations. As she turned back, she saw a couple who were sitting at a table on the other side of the room. It was Ian, and with him Miss Williams, the secretary from school.

She felt her cheeks burn and then drain. No wonder Ian had been cool towards her. He was taking the secretary out. She wondered how long this had been going on. It wasn't so many weeks since they had gone to Trentham together and he certainly wasn't the type who go out with more than one female at a time.

'What's wrong?' asked Alistair, seeing her pale face.

'Nothing. Sorry. Maybe I moved too quickly when I turned round. I just felt a little dizzy.'

'I'll take you home right away. You've had a busy time and must be exhausted. I should have been more thoughtful and left this evening out till after you'd broken up from school.'

'I am tired and the weather is awful. Thank you. You've been very kind and it was a lovely meal.'

They got up to leave and Ian smiled at her in a strange way. She could hardly walk out without speaking but felt extremely uncomfortable. She couldn't explain it. After all, they were both free agents and there were no ties. All the same, she felt her dreams slipping away and a huge sense of loss. She had always felt that she and Ian would somehow overcome the difficulties and everything would end happily. Stupid romantic idiot that she was.

'I, er, hope you're enjoying your evening,' she muttered as they went past Ian and his companion. How could he go out with Miss Williams? She was older than him and frankly, a bit dowdy. She walked on without stopping to introduce Alistair and felt as if their eyes were burning into her rear.

'Who was that?' Alistair asked. 'I thought you were going to introduce us for one brief moment. But I suppose you're ashamed of me.'

'Don't be silly. I just want to get home before the weather gets even worse.'

'That was clearly someone who upset you. I bet you like him and he was with someone else. I'm right, aren't I?' She said nothing, but her looks must have given her away. 'Why waste time on someone who's not interested when you can have me, all ready, willing and able?'

It was a dreadful drive home. It was now snowing and the roads were icy. Lucy could think of nothing but seeing Ian and Miss Williams together. Fortunately, Alistair was having to concentrate hard and didn't mind the silence.

'This is horrible,' he moaned. 'Still, not much further.' They were greatly relieved when they reached home. 'I had a lovely evening. Thank you. Now, you see how well we can get on together? Do you think we might spend more time together? I love you, Lucy.'

'Oh, Alistair, I'm sorry. It was a nice evening, but I can't. I don't want to spend time together when I can see no future for us.'

'But there will never be anyone else for me. You're the only person I have ever loved and the only girl I'd ever want to marry. Please, Lucy . . . '

'I'm not sure how to get it across to you,' she said desperately. 'You seem to ignore whatever I say.' Then she had an inspiration. 'Actually, I'm seeing someone else and in fact, I'm rather hoping we might get engaged soon. So you see, there really is no point in coming over again. Sorry.'

'Well, well. I wonder why your mother didn't say anything? But perhaps she doesn't know yet. Congratulations. Who's the lucky man? Someone you met recently? Not that creep from the wedding? Anne's brother, wasn't it?'

'No, certainly not Joe. It's . . . he's someone I've known for a while, actually. Local chap.'

'Whatever. You are a very bad liar, Lucy, but that makes you all the more endearing. If it was that man in the restaurant, seems to me you're backing a loser. He clearly has someone else.' He looked at her but she made no further comment. 'Bye then. Have a nice Christmas. Be in touch.' He peeped the horn as he drove away and gave her a wave and blew her a kiss. She frowned and shook her head in frustration. Cold and damp for the second time that day, she opened the door and went inside.

'You're home early,' Sylvia said. 'Good evening?'

'Sort of. Nice meal.'

'But?'

'Oh, Mum, it was awful. I felt so mean. Alistair couldn't have been nicer. He was polite and tried to do every-thing right. The meal was delicious.'

'But you don't care for him and now you feel guilty.'

'Well yes. But there's more. Ian and Miss Williams, the school secretary were in the restaurant. I don't know how I ever could have thought he might care for me. It can't have been going on for that long, with Miss Williams, I mean. Certainly not when he took me to Trentham. He wouldn't do that. He was really upset when we met Joe because Joe suggested we were close. Oh Mum, what a mess.'

'There's nothing to be gained by moping. Do you want anything before you go to bed?' Lucy shook her head. 'Right well, you'd better get yourself off to bed. Just think, this time tomorrow, you'll have completed your first full term as a teacher. Well done. I'm so proud of you.'

'Nearly Christmas and I haven't done a scrap of shopping. How about we go up to Hanley on Thursday? Have a blitz on the shops.'

'All right. You're on. Bet it'll be

127

crowded though.'

The last day of term was something of an anti-climax. Many of the children stayed away and the ones who were there were over excited and didn't want to do anything. They were to finish early with a full school assembly at the end of the day. They were going to sing carols and have some readings and Lucy was quite looking forward to it. She had seen Ian in passing and there had been no chance to speak. After the promising start to the term, things had certainly changed. Perhaps the new term might mean they could at least be on speaking terms again.

It was a relaxing time over the holidays. Lucy did a bit of school work to prepare for the coming term, but mostly enjoyed her break. Jim had been a delightful companion over Christmas Day and she felt happy for her mother. They seemed very well suited and as he was a widower too, they shared a knowledge of what it was like to be lonely.

Her mother must have been very lost during the years she had been away at college and Lucy once more felt pangs of guilt that she had been oblivious to the huge changes in Sylvia's life.

All too soon, it was January the sixth and the start of the new term. There was a staff meeting at the beginning of the first day and her chance to meet the rest of her colleagues again.

Ian came to sit next to her and once she had calmed down the thumping of her heart, she spoke quietly to him.

'Have a good break?' she asked fatuously. How cool was that, she thought. Stupid woman.

'Busy,' he replied. 'You?'

'Quiet. Nice chance to slob around and rest.'

The Head called the meeting to order and spoke about plans for the coming term. He mentioned a number of dates, including a Governor's meeting for which he nodded specifically at her. She dutifully wrote it down in her notebook, assuming he expected a tea party once more.

She glanced at Ian, remembering the last meeting and what had happened after it, but he made no sign of recognition. The memory of seeing him with Miss Williams came into her mind and she glanced at the school secretary. She seemed to be engrossed writing the notes of the meeting and she had scarcely even looked across at Ian. If they really were going out together, they were being extremely discreet about it.

'Now finally,' the Head droned on. 'We have had a request to start some dancing lessons. It will be after school on a Monday night and Miss Hodges and Mr Bailey will conduct the sessions, but I'm sure they would appreciate some support from any other members of staff willing to stay behind. I'm sure you'll all agree that after their demonstration at the school party, they are well suited to this task.' There was a murmur of assent from the rest of the staff.

Lucy felt her cheeks burning and turned to look at Ian. He looked as uncomfortable as she felt.

'Did you know anything about this?'

'No more than you did. Apart from Gary suggesting it at the time, it's never been mentioned to me.'

'Can he do this? The Head I mean. Can he insist we take this on?'

'Officially, no. But it would look good on your record if you agree to it and bad for your probationary year if you don't.'

'So are you willing to give it a go? Even if you are very busy?'

'I suppose so. If you want to do it.' She thought for a moment. There was nothing she would like more than whirling around a dance floor with this man, but would the proximity to someone she cared about be too much to handle? Especially knowing he was going out with someone else.

'Ok then. We'll see how it goes. How do we go about it, do you reckon?'

'We could discuss it over coffee later.'

'That would be nice. Like old times,' she added without thinking.

'Yes, well I've been very busy.'

The school day began and soon Lucy and her colleagues were organising their groups as if they had never been away. By lunchtime, she felt as if the Christmas break had never happened.

She and Ian had barely started to discuss the new dancing classes, when break was over. They agreed to meet again the next day. She had rather mixed feelings. Much as she wanted to share this time with him, it could be tricky now she had acknowledged she really did hold feelings for him.

'I can't really refuse,' she explained to her mother that evening, 'because it would look bad for my probationary status. Not that I want to say no, anyhow. I think it might be fun and the children were enthusiastic too.'

'You'll just have to make the most of it then, won't you, love? Oh, by the way, I heard from the telephone people. They can put one in within six weeks. Not bad as some areas have a waiting list of months.'

132

'Might be nice to be able to contact you, I must say. We just don't tell anyone we don't want to hear from.'

'Like your Auntie Elsie for instance?' They both giggled.

'Especially Auntie Elsie. She'd never be off the phone telling you all her woes and how her *screwmatics* were playing up.'

'She really enjoys her bad health that one. Poor old thing. S'pose she's really just lonely.'

'I'm glad you've got Jim around, Mum. You won't feel so lonely when I'm out. Must have been awful when I was away being so busy with my own stuff all the time and you were on your own here.'

'I'm all right. But I'm glad you like Jim. I'm getting quite fond of him, I must admit.' Lucy stared at her Mum in surprise. She rarely said anything about her own feelings. She squeezed Sylvia's hand and smiled.

'I'd better do some work now. What are we having for supper?'

'Lamb chops. The butcher had some beauties in today. Thought we'd treat ourselves. An hour do you?'

'Great.'

She worked on her lesson plans for the next couple of days. It was much easier now she had got into the swing of things and her organisation of her classes was starting to become second nature. To begin with, she made cards to say what time the various processes needed to be completed.

10.15. All pastry completed and left to relax before rolling.

10.40. Pies must be in oven.

Now she could manage with her timings in the plan itself. Other teachers would never understand the complexity of getting everything organised to such an extent. They mostly had to cope with just finishing an exercise in a book and handing it in. If things weren't properly cooked by the end of the lesson, they couldn't be taken home. Once she had finished, she gave thought to the dancing class problem.

Ian had told her there were records available for the various dances and they'd got as far as planning to book the hall with the caretaker for an hour after school on Mondays. She made a decision. If they were to be professional about it, she needed to discuss the more personal matters with Ian. Miss Williams coming at the top of the list.

Granted, Ian's personal life was nothing to do with her, but she wanted to be certain there could be no embarrassment caused. Lucy planned to tackle him the next day after school. It was hopeless to try and talk much during the day, especially as Marion would be there tomorrow.

'Supper's ready,' Sylvia called.

'On my way,' Lucy replied, happier now she had made her decision.

8

When the end of the school day finally arrived, Lucy felt in a state of nerves. She finished clearing up her room and waited till the washing was finished. It was an elderly single tub machine and she had to rinse and mangle all the tea towels and put them on the clothes horse to dry overnight, ready for the next day. She longed for a spin dryer to ease the burden and planned to request one the next time she was in touch with the advisor. Usually, she managed to get the washing done towards the end of the lesson but it had been a hectic session this afternoon.

At least it meant that all of Ian's group would have left by the time she went over for her chat. He was staying in school tonight as it was his evening class later on. Plucking up her courage, she locked the doors and went across the playground to the woodwork room.

She tapped on the door and turned the handle. It was locked. She cursed, thinking he must have gone over to the main building. But she could hear music playing and definitely, the sound of voices. She knocked again, thinking he must have the radio on. She was turning away when the door was opened.

'Oh, hi. It's you.'

'Sorry. I wondered if there was a chance to talk? Days never seem to have any spare time.'

'Oh. Well, er . . . if you like. You'd better come in.' He seemed uncomfortable and Lucy hesitated before following him into the room. She stopped in her tracks when she saw the scene. One of the usually grubby benches was covered with a table cloth.

There were plates of chicken and salad and two dishes of fruit salad set out. Miss Williams was sitting on a stool, looking distinctly unhappy at the intrusion. She nodded but her face showed great annoyance.

'Oh, I'm so sorry. I didn't realise. I'll go.'

'No, really, it's quite all right,' Ian was saying.

'I'm interrupting your . . . er . . . your meal. It'll keep.' She turned and almost ran out of the room.

How could she have been so stupid as to think someone like Ian wouldn't have a relationship?

He was probably the most attractive man she had ever known. Clearly, Miss Williams thought he was something special and had been furious at Lucy's interruption to their tea party.

She collected her bags and went along the high street to catch her train home. Blast, she muttered as she realised the school keys were still in her pocket. Too bad. She wouldn't go back for anything now.

'Why can't I be happy with someone who actually likes me?' she moaned to her mother. 'I always choose the wrong man. Poor old Alistair is there wanting to spend time with me. Joe seemed to like me.'

'The right one will come along sometime. And don't settle for anything you consider to be second best. From what you told me, Joe is there for the good times and would be a disaster as a permanent boyfriend. You'd never be able to trust him. I suspect Alistair is still finding his feet in the world and wants support while he's doing it. He's been spoilt all his life by wealthy family and now he's on his own, he doesn't like it.'

'What a wise old bird you are, Mum,' Lucy said fondly. 'You're absolutely right. And I don't really know Ian at all, do I? I'm drawn by a handsome face and what seems like a nice personality. But I hardly know anything about his background or hobbies or his plans. But he's a cracking dancer,' she added with a grin.

'Then enjoy your dancing classes with him and try to forget about the rest. Don't look at me like that. Enjoy what you can and if anything else is meant to happen, it will.'

'OK. But I think I need to avoid seeing too much of him. Not easy under the circumstances, but I guess it can work. Thanks, Mum.'

'Will you be all right on your own this evening? Only Jim's taking me out to the cinema. You could come as well if you wanted to. We're going to see *West Side Story*. I'm not sure if I'm going to like it but still, it'll make a change.'

'There's no way I'm going to play gooseberry to my own mother. You enjoy it and if it's good, I might go at the weekend. Actually, it's about time I met up with some of the old crowd. I might see if Anne's doing anything. I'll walk along to the phone box later and give her a call. Be nice when we've got our own phone, won't it?'

'Thought you were negative about it.'

'I can see very many advantages,' Lucy laughed.

Ian came over to her room the next morning.

'I'm sorry about yesterday,' he said. 'Was there something special you wanted to talk about?'

'No. Just trying to sort out these wretched dancing classes.'

'I should explain. About Jenny. Jenny Williams.'

'Don't be silly, Ian. You don't have to explain anything to me. What you do in your private life is nothing to do with me.'

'But I . . . '

'Let's plan our strategy,' she put in before he could say any more. 'We're fixed on Monday evenings for an hour.'

'If you like. But you ought to listen to me.'

'I suggest we start with a sort of free for all and then try to sort out some basic steps, once we see how bad they are. We can then demonstrate how it fits into the rhythm and then they can try it. We can take turns in partnering the kids.' She spoke quickly, not giving him the chance to speak. She didn't want to hear confirmed what she suspected. Ian nodded and gave up whatever he wanted to say.

They mapped out the first session and were all set to begin the following week.

'I really don't know how this will go, but at least we're making the attempt. At least the Head can't complain, can he?' Lucy said.

Quite a crowd of pupils arrived in the hall for the first session and they all seemed to enjoy it. The feedback the following day was very positive, but how the attendance for the rest of term would go, they had to wait and see.

'Are you and Mr Bailey going out, Miss?' one of the girls asked the next day. 'Only you danced real well together. As if you're used to it.'

'Not that it's any of your business, but no, we're not going out. He's a very good dancer and makes it easy to follow him.'

'You should go out with him, Miss. He's so good looking and he obviously likes you.'

Lucy found herself blushing to the roots of her hair. She was at a loss about what to say. Clearly she had been too open with her pupils and she should be much more aloof.

They really shouldn't be saying things like that to her but she wasn't so very much older than them. In some ways, it was flattering that they felt able to talk to her on such terms but she could just imagine what the Head might think of it.

'Enough chat. You have work to do.' She soon got them involved in their tasks and pretended not to notice the nudges and smirks when Ian arrived for his coffee.

'What's up with them?' Ian asked, as the giggling bunch of girls went out past him.

'Too many rampant hormones after the dancing class,' she fibbed. 'I think they all want to dance with you next week.'

'Oh dear. And to think I was worried about you. Went well though, didn't it?'

'Time will tell.'

One break later in the week, a deputation of boys came across from Ian's group.

'Please, Miss, we wondered if you'd start a cookery club for the boys? Some of us want to learn to cook stuff and its not fair that only the girls get to do it.'

'That sounds like a great idea,' Lucy replied happily. She had often complained that only the girls took cookery and the boys woodwork. She always hoped there could be some sort of exchange of subjects, but it was always a world of boy's subjects and girls subjects. 'I'll have to see the Head of course and get his permission. But I like the idea.'

'Thanks, Miss. Will you teach us how to make snake and kidney pie cos I've got a snake?'

To Lucy's horror, the wretched boy held up a grass snake he'd just caught out in the playground. She had a total phobia about snakes and clutched the end of her desk, feeling as if she might faint at any moment. In as loud a voice as she could muster, she said, 'Get that thing out of here. This is a cookery room, not a zoo.'

Fortunately, he obeyed and left. Once it was out of sight, she took a deep breath to steady herself. 'I am not amused,' she told the remaining boys. 'Was this just a prank to see my reaction?'

'No, Miss. Honest. We told him not to bring it in. We do want some lessons, please.'

'All right then. I'll speak to the Head tomorrow, but make sure that boy knows I will not tolerate stupid behaviour.'

'Yes, Miss. Thanks, Miss.' They trooped out.

'Oh, Miss, wasn't that awful? You were very brave when he showed you that snake. I nearly screamed.' The girl was looking slightly shaken.

'So did I,' Lucy told her. 'I hate them.' The class giggled mildly. Another one spoke.

'Please, Miss, my brother would like to cook. He's going to be a chef. Can I tell him about your cooking club?'

'Better wait till it's official. And there will have to be a limit on who comes. I can't have more than fifteen in this room.'

The Head seemed disinterested in her project, but told her to ask the caretaker if he was willing to have the room open late. It seemed slightly odd to her that it was the caretaker who'd say yea or nay to what was after all, part of the education system.

The cookery club for boys was planned as a six-week trial. It was over-subscribed and she had to turn away a number of pupils. Ian told her it was bound to work as the boys would enjoy being taught by a pretty young woman. She had blushed at his words but felt a warm glow of pleasure.

With careful organisation, she managed to complete each of the classes in just over an hour, but it meant she had a limited range of dishes she could cook with the boys. After six weeks, it was deemed a great success and another group was started.

Days and weeks went by with a hectic work load keeping Lucy busy. She had a couple of visits from the advisory staff and received good feedback from them.

Apart from producing teas for the Governor's meetings, she seemed to have little personal contact with the Head. Not that she was worried by this, but she did think he might have little idea of her abilities as a teacher and was concerned about her final report as the end of the year came closer.

Alistair had taken the hint and had left her alone, despite his declarations of love. In fact, her social life still seemed non-existent and she hadn't even made plans for any sort of holiday later in the summer.

Ian had been friendly enough but after walking in on him and Miss Williams, she had never even tried to see him again after school. They maintained a cool, somewhat distant relationship, much as she hated doing it. But keeping things on a fairly superficial level was so much easier.

With only two weeks to go to the end of term, one of the staff came round with an envelope collecting money for a wedding present for Miss Williams. Lucy felt a cold shiver run through her. How on earth could things have got this far without Ian saying a single thing?

She and Ian saw each other every day and she'd really believed they were close enough for him to have confided in her. She looked in her bag and took some money out of her purse to put in the envelope.

'Is that all right?' she asked her colleague, unsure of how much was expected.

'Course. Not as if she was a major staff member anyway. These envelopes seem to go round so often when people leave or get married or something. Thanks.'

'But Ian's a major staff member,' she said to the retreating figure but she had not been heard. She wondered how many of the staff had been invited to the wedding. Clearly she was not among the chosen few. She felt a little disappointed in a way, but watching him get married would have been a new form of torture.

She had barely recovered from the shock of the impending wedding when she saw the Head coming down the path towards her room. She quickly glanced round to see that it was tidy and tossed a couple of dirty tea-towels into the washer.

'Miss Hodges,' the Head said as he walked into the room. 'Settled in well now?'

'Erm, yes thank you,' she muttered, startled by his question. 'The room's much better than when I arrived, but there's still a few problems that need sorting out.'

'I'm sure there are. Well, you've made an excellent beginning to your career. I'm here to tell you that you have passed your probationary year with flying colours. You are well organised and the students all seem to like you. I've been pleased by the way you have taken on extra responsibilities. That's it. Congratulations. I have written to the appropriate authorities with my report on your work.'

'Thank you, Sir,' she mumbled. 'Thank you very much. I was a bit worried that you hadn't been over to see my class and that perhaps you'd forgotten.'

'Course not. I'm always aware of what is going on in my school. Mr Bailey has also answered a few of my questions about the way things were going. Have a good holiday. You've earned it.' He turned and left the room as Lucy stood almost open-mouthed at the brief visit.

She'd done it. She was now fully qualified and on equal terms with everyone else. She did a little dance of joy round the tables and laughed out loud. She must go and thank Ian for his input. Clearly, as the Head had never seen her working, Ian must be responsible for her good report.

She was about to go out of the room when she remembered Miss Williams and the wedding. Along with her thanks for his good report of her, she probably needed to congratulate him.

Though she had spent the months trying not to think of him as anything but another colleague, she knew deep inside that she did truly love him. Each time he was near to her she felt her pulse racing and a sudden leap of her stomach when she saw him unexpectedly. She still cursed Joe over and over for giving the impression that she had some sort of reputation.

Alistair's arrival on the scene at inopportune moments hadn't helped either. What a mess. But now it was all over. It was too late. Her feelings had to be squashed away somewhere and never taken out again for further examination.

Next term was going to be very difficult if they were continually thrown together with dancing classes and cosy little cups of coffee over break. She took a deep breath and locked the doors. It was raining slightly, but she knew she must face up to things and trembling just a little she knocked on Ian's door.

'Oh, hi. Do you want a coffee? I have got a kettle and a couple of mugs, but I don't suppose they quite pass your high standards of hygiene.'

'Thanks. I'm sure it will be fine.' She felt awkward and watched silently as he went about his task.

'It's my emergency coffee, for when I can't get over to you.'

'I see. I hadn't realised. Actually, I came to thank you.'

'Oh? For what?'

'The Head's just been across to tell me my probationary year is over and that I have passed. He was quite complimentary in fact.'

'Well done you,' he said happily, grabbing her round the waist and twirling her round. 'So all the extras did it for you? Dancing classes, cookery classes and good quality teaching.'

'He said you'd put in a good report and I'd never even realised you were watching me.'

'Hardly. No, he merely asked me how I thought you were doing and I told him the truth. You're a good teacher. Popular with the kids and a very hard worker. What more could anyone ask.'

'Thank you,' she said quietly, feeling almost embarrassed by his praise and still trying to recover from the exhilaration of his greeting. What a lovely man he was.

'One coffee. Black, I'm afraid. Can't run to milk. And you don't take sugar, do you?'

'Thanks. That's fine. Erm . . . there's something else. I understand congratulations are in order.'

'Oh. I thought nobody knew. Thanks anyway. It's been a hard slog but worth it in the end.'

Lucy frowned. What an odd choice of words.

'I'm sorry? What do you mean?'

'A lot of hard work. Trying to fit it in around the edges of teaching and not having any typing skills anyway.'

'I'm completely lost. Exactly what are you talking about?'

'What are you talking about?'

'Your marriage.'

'My what?' he almost shouted.

'Your wedding.'

'Oh yes? And when is this supposed to be taking place?'

'Well, soon, I suppose.'

'Really. What gives you that idea?' He sounded almost angry.

'A collection's being made.'

'And exactly who am I supposed to be marrying?'

'Miss Williams?' she almost whispered.

He burst out laughing and pulled her towards him.

'I'm not marrying Miss Williams or anyone else. Well, I confess I do hope to marry one day, but I haven't asked her yet. But why on earth do you think I'd marry Miss Williams?'

'You took her out to dinner. And I walked in on you one day. I'll never forget the look on her face when I arrived. She looked as if she could kill me.'

'Oh heavens,' he said with a laugh. 'I wondered why you'd gone so cold and unapproachable.' He looked serious again. 'I assumed you were seeing that man again and I wasn't going to stand a chance. Sorry, but I don't want to share, when it comes to loving someone.'

'Well, you don't love me, do you?'

'Haven't been given the chance to get to know you well enough.'

Lucy swallowed hard to try and calm her nerves. She was trembling slightly but for a whole new reason.

'Not my fault,' she whispered.

9

As Lucy sat on the train for her short journey home, she was bathed in a glow of happiness. How quickly emotions could turn from deep depression to a high cloud of good cheer.

Their coffee had been left to grow cold and undrinkable as they had kissed, held each other and finally made plans for a meal out together later that evening. Ian needed to finish off some work and so hadn't offered her a lift home. She had phoned her mother from the station call box to say she was going out for the evening and didn't want a meal. Sylvia had sounded relieved and said she too was going out.

'Tell you everything when I get there. Bye.'

She remembered something as she thought of their conversation. When she had congratulated Ian, he'd said thanks and that he didn't realise she knew. What on earth was he on about? She'd been thinking of her mistake about the wedding but clearly, there was something else going on. She must remember to ask during the evening.

But now, there was the serious problem of what to wear. Her wardrobe was in grave need of replenishment. She was planning to give it a major overhaul and buy some new things during the school holidays. It was about the only thing she had actually planned to do during the summer break.

'What a day,' she told her mother. 'But I've passed my probationary year with flying colours and Ian's not getting married after all. He's asked me out this evening and oh, Mum, I'm so happy.' She swung her mother round just as Ian had done with her earlier.

'I didn't know he was getting married.'

'Nor did I, till someone came round collecting for a present. I assumed he was marrying Miss Williams, but I was wrong. I'm not sure why he was even spending so much time with her, but I intend to find out this evening. Now I have to find something interesting to wear. I really need to sort out my wardrobe.'

She bounced upstairs and Sylvia smiled, shaking her head. When Lucy was happy, the whole place seemed to be affected. But she was delighted for her daughter. She had been working far too hard and enjoying life much too little of late. But Sylvia had some news of her own. She would save it for another time. There was no urgency.

When Ian arrived, she invited him in to see her mother.

'I'm sorry, we shouldn't stay long. I know that sounds rude, but I booked a table and we're already slightly late. I took longer to finish off at work than I intended.'

'No problem. I'm going out in a minute anyway and still have to finish getting ready. Have a lovely evening, you two.'

'We will,' said Lucy happily.

'You look lovely,' Ian told her as he shut the car door behind her.

'Where are we going?' she asked.

'Little pub with a nice restaurant out at Moddershall. It's only a small place, but I've heard the food's good.'

'Great.' It was a short drive through the country lanes and it had turned into a beautiful summer evening. 'Funny,' she said. 'Everyone thinks of Staffordshire as an industrial country with lots of mining and pottery factories belching out smoke. But really, it's very rural and very green and pretty.'

'I'm always surprised at the speed you leave the industry behind and find yourself in the country. And many of the potteries were built alongside the canals, so there's always grass growing right in the middle of the towns. Here we are. The car park's round to the side.'

'Tell me, why did you say thank you when I congratulated you?'

'I assumed you'd found out about my book.'

'Book?'

'Yes. I've been writing a technical book on woodworking. A sort of teaching manual. I was approached by a distant relative of mine who works in a publishing company. That's why I've been so busy all year. But it was finished a little while back and I've now heard it's been accepted. It's all going ahead.'

'And that's why you were seeing so much of Miss Williams?'

'Yes, of course. She was typing it all up for me. I can't type to save my life so she offered. I did all the diagrams and stuff and wrote out the text by hand. You know what my writing's like. She struggled through it all and I took her out for a thank you meal after she did the first draft. She then had to start again on the second draft after the publishers had seen it and suggested changes.'

'I see. And the picnics in your room? I only walked in on the one, but I did see her going into your room with a basket on several other occasions.'

'That was becoming difficult. I found it more than a little embarrassing, especially as she was engaged to someone else. They hadn't been getting on and she'd taken to coming to confide in me. Thought if she brought a meal along to this poor starving bachelor, something more exciting might develop. I couldn't really do much about it when she continued to do so much typing for me. She would never take any money for it either.'

'How strange. But now she's getting married after all.'

'All the time, I really wanted to spent some time with you. But when I saw you with someone else and we met that other guy, I assumed you wouldn't be interested in me. Why would you? You had plenty of attention from other men.'

'What a pair of idiots. I've been desperately trying to hide the fact that I'd fallen in love with you, for months.' She stopped, her fork halfway to her mouth as she realised what she'd said.

'Sorry. Mouth was engaged before brain.' Her face was fiery red and she shivered despite the heat.

'Would you mind repeating that?' he asked.

'No. Certainly not. Sorry.'

'We truly are a pair of idiots. I fell in love with you when we first went to Trentham. I was devastated when we met that bloke who claimed you'd been a swinging sixties sort of girl. I couldn't bear it and had to get away.'

'All that time we wasted,' she said softly.

'Not altogether wasted. At least I managed to finish my book. I'd never have managed it with you to distract me. I seem to have been working on it nearly every weekend for as long as I can remember.' He took her hand and gently kissed her fingertips.

'As I said to Mum, what a day this has been. Bit like a roller coaster of emotions.'

They finished the meal and went back to his car. He slid an arm along the back of her seat and drew her close.

His lips found hers and she felt as if she was floating on air.

'You're beautiful, Miss Hodges.'

'Thank you, Mr Bailey. You're not short in the looks department yourself. Half of the fourth years think they're in love with you.' She stroked his cheek with her fingers and smiled.

She could never remember feeling so happy before.

'Did you mean it when you said you loved me?'

'I did. And did you mean it?'

'No doubt about it.'

'Let's go home and I'll make you some coffee. Don't know when Mum'll be back but you're all right with it, if she's home?'

'Course. I need to get to know her too.'

★   ★   ★

They had the cottage to themselves and he followed her into the kitchen as she made coffee.

'I was thinking,' he said. 'Have you got any plans for the holidays?'

'Only a major sort out of my wardrobe. And the planning for the next school year of course. We're going to be doing GCEs next year.'

'Forget about work for five minutes, will you? I was wondering if we might have a holiday together? I desperately need a break and suggest that you do too. I have an aunt who lives on Anglesey. She runs a boarding house and I'm sure she'll have a couple of rooms still available for a week or two.'

'Wow, that sounds great. I haven't been there since I was a kid. Only thing is, it's a bit hard on my mum.'

'Think about it. If you'd like to go, let me know as soon as you can or she'll get booked up.'

They chatted for another hour, discovering things about each other that they had both wanted to ask for months but always felt inhibited.

'How could we have gone so long without knowing what the other was thinking?' he asked.

'Neither of us wanted to look foolish. We both had the wrong ends of sticks and well, I for one didn't want to hear a truth I might not like.' He nodded agreement.

'Would you come to Jenny's wedding with me? I was invited and decided I wouldn't go on my own. Always hate being on my own at those sort of affairs. But if you were with me, I'd feel much happier.'

'If you're sure she won't mind. I don't think she likes me very much.'

'Jealous, that's all. But it is her wedding. She can't possibly feel jealous on that day of all days.'

'OK, then. When is it?'

'Two weeks after we break up. We could have our holiday first and come back for the wedding or go away afterwards. Heavens, I'd better get going or I'll never make it in time for school tomorrow.'

'I'll talk to Mum when she gets back and let you know tomorrow.'

'Thank you for a wonderful evening.'

'It's going to be very difficult in school, not to let anyone see how I feel about you.'

'We must keep it a secret though. Remember what the Head said that time after the Governor's meeting?'

'Maybe we'll keep it quiet for now.' He kissed her once more and then left.

★   ★   ★

She hugged herself, an idiotic grin of pleasure on her face. She washed the coffee cups and could hardly wait for her mother to return. It was getting close to midnight when she heard the car stop.

She went to the door and opened it. Jim and her mother were kissing each other and didn't even notice her standing there.

She backed into the house and pushed the door to. She felt slightly shocked and shook herself. Somehow, she never thought of her mother and a man actually kissing each other. How naïve could she be?

Her mother was still a relatively young woman and, of course, she and Jim would want to be close. All the same, it was something of a surprise to her. She must learn not to be so self-centred, just as she had been before when she was away at college.

Did anyone ever think of their parents as people and not just parents? It must happen at some point and maybe everyone felt this same sense of shock.

'You're still up,' Sylvia commented. 'How was your evening?'

'Wonderful. He's such a wonderful man and I'm so happy.' She was about to launch into her plans for a holiday but made herself stop. 'What about your evening?'

'Great,' she said briefly. 'Tell me all about it.'

'I want to hear about you. It's time I noticed someone other than myself,' Lucy replied.

'Oh, darling. Being all about yourself is traditional amongst young people.'

'Well, it's time I grew up. You and Jim are getting very close, aren't you?'

'Actually, he's asked me to marry him. How would you feel about that?'

'Oh, Mum, that's great. Really great. I'm delighted for you.'

'You're sure you're not upset by the thought? I mean it's hardly as if someone was replacing your father after all these years.'

'Course it isn't. I can hardly remember Dad. I was only tiny when he died. It's well past time you found your own happiness.'

'Thank you, love. I'll say yes then, shall I?'

'You mean you haven't?'

'Course not. Not till I'd spoken to you first.'

'Oh, Mum. Do you ever stop being a mum and putting your children first?'

'I don't suppose so. But, you tell me about your evening now.'

They talked into the night. Wedding

plans were discussed and holidays in Anglesey. Where they would live and a whole heap of things.

'I'm never going to be up in the morning if I don't get just a little sleep. Not that I expect to sleep. I'm too excited.'

'Isn't it all exciting? As you said, what a day.'

'It's already tomorrow. I haven't even thought what I'm doing yet. The kids are already as high as kites and there's still almost two weeks to go before the end of term.'

★   ★   ★

Lucy could scarcely believe it was time to get up when the alarm went off after so little sleep, she felt heavy and lethargic, but she struggled through a mug of tea and the toast her mother insisted she ate and almost had to run to catch her train.

The fifteen minute journey gave her time to reflect on the previous day. Her mother and Jim planned to marry as soon as they could arrange everything. There was little point in waiting. If she had her holiday with Ian early in the holidays, they could make plans for the wedding when she got back.

On the other hand, it might be nice to make all the preparations before they went away so they could relax. She almost stayed on the train, so busy was she with her thoughts and plans. She could hardly wait to see Ian again and tell him the latest news.

There was a lot of chatter coming from the staff room. Clearly, it wasn't only the children who were high as kites. She went in and several people called out congratulations. She wasn't sure why and looked for Ian. He was grinning.

'Told them you'd passed your probationary year.'

'And about his book. We'll all have to bow to him now he's a published author.'

'I'm not actually published yet. But

you can bow anyway. I might enjoy that.'

'And a little bird tells us you and Ian are walking out, as they used to say.'

Lucy blushed and looked again at Ian. He was still smiling.

'Can't keep anything secret in this place.'

'But I thought we weren't going to tell anyone,' she protested.

'When he's walking round with an idiotic grin on his face, I've known him long enough to know there's something going on. Can't keep secrets from Uncle Gary. Well done the pair of you. I'm pleased for you both.'

'Well, thanks, but please keep quiet about it in front of you-know-who.' She nodded towards the Head's office door.

'What's it got to do with him?' Gary asked.

Lucy told him about the unfortunate incident after the Governor's meeting.

He grinned. 'You sly old thing,' he said pushing a friendly punch towards Ian's middle. 'But he's no right to stop you seeing each other outside school, whether or not you work together. He's a silly man who wanted to keep you in his power till you'd completed your year. Now you've done it.'

'So we have your permission to go on holiday, do we Gary?'

'Of course. Just make sure you enjoy it. And Lucy, just watch him. I'll have to give you a few tips on how to handle him.'

'Oh, I think I know how to do that.' She smiled. 'Now, I'd better go and do some teaching.'

* * *

They decided to go on holiday for the first week of the summer break and possibly stay on a few days into the second week.

They had agreed to return for Miss William's wedding, though neither of them were exactly keen on attending.

Sylvia and Jim had decided on the last Saturday in August for their day. It would be a small affair with just a few close friends and family being invited.

Even so, Lucy intended that everything should be perfect and was organising everything to the last detail, even before the term had ended. Sylvia had protested.

'You'll be making lesson plans for us next. Every second of the day organised in detail.'

'Oh Mum, I'm sorry. I'm taking over, aren't I? I just want it all to be perfect for you. And if I leave it all till we get back from our trip to Anglesey, I shall be panicking the whole week I'm away.'

'Organise away, love. I don't mind really. But there will only be a dozen or so, of us. It's not exactly a Royal wedding of the year. And I do appreciate your motives.'

'But really, I'd like you to get ready for your own holiday first. You were going to renovate your wardrobe, if I remember rightly.'

'No time. I'll just have a trip to Hanley at the weekend. Buy some new stuff and resist the fabric shops.'

'Wow. That will be a first, love. I can't

actually remember when you went out and bought yourself some ready made clothes.'

'You could come too and we could look at wedding outfits.'

'I'm not bothering with anything too special. I'm sure there's something in my wardrobe . . . '

'And let Jim think he's not special enough to merit a new outfit? I don't think so. You're going to look totally spectacular on your wedding day.'

'We'll see. But all right. I'll come with you on Saturday. We haven't had a day out together for ages.'

* * *

For possibly the first time in her life, Lucy had some money of her own saved. She had spent very little on herself over the year and was ready to have a spending spree.

As well as buying some new clothes for herself, she wanted to buy something special for her mum. Something extravagant and impractical to show her how much she appreciated her support over the past year.

None of it had been particularly easy but now, they both had something to celebrate. She was also determined to buy herself an electric sewing machine but that might have to wait until she had the means of getting it home. Perhaps she might persuade Ian to drive her and then it would be easy. But today, it was a day for the two of them.

They looked at dresses and jackets suitable for weddings, but Sylvia really couldn't decide on anything. It was too soon to buy things yet, she had protested.

'We could come over again nearer the time. We'll know more what the weather's doing by then.'

Her mother was adamant and Lucy could not persuade her to change her mind and so she concentrated on her own things. She bought several new tops and a couple of pairs of trousers and unable to resist, two lengths of fabric to make summer dresses.

'There, I knew you wouldn't spend out on new dresses. You always know what you want and can never find exactly the right thing. You were always the same, even when you were little.'

'Actually, Mum, I'm going to buy an electric sewing machine, so I needed some fabric to practice on. All right? Shall we go and look at them now and then maybe I can get Ian to drive me over to collect it?'

They watched the demonstration in the shop and very quickly, Lucy decided on the model she wanted. She wrote out the cheque and smiled at her mother.

'Little does it know how hard it's going to work during its life,' she said. She was delighted to discover that the shop would actually deliver the machine and they fixed on the following Wednesday.

'That's fantastic. I shall have time to make my dresses in time for the holiday. Now, we're going into Hunt-batch's. They've got some things I need to buy.'

'Exactly what do you want from there?'

'You'll see.' Lucy had decided on a china figurine, a Royal Doulton lady that her mother had once cherished and which Lucy had broken one day when she was little. She had never forgotten the look on Sylvia's face when it lay on the hearth in a hundred tiny pieces.

'Sorry, Mummy. Mummy mend it?' she had said.

'No love. It's too badly broken to be able to fix it. But it was an accident and you didn't mean to break it.'

'Didn't mean to break it,' Lucy had repeated.

They went into the department store and she led her mother to the china section. Fortunately, the figurine was still in production and there she was, standing on the shelf. Sylvia looked at it.

'I had one of those,' she said softly.

'I know. And I broke it. Now I'm replacing it.'

'Don't be silly darling. It's much too expensive.'

'Nonsense. Since when did anything I ever want prove too expensive? You always managed it somehow and this is just a tiny token of my gratitude to you for all you've done for me.'

'The original was a wedding present from your granny. That's why it was special.'

'OK. This is a little wedding present from me and it's also very special.' Tearfully, her mother accepted the wrapped parcel from the sales assistant and carried it carefully out of the shop.

'Thank you, darling. It's very kind of you. I shall treasure this one just as much. More probably, because of your thoughtfulness.'

'Yes, well I hope you don't break that one.' They both laughed, and the emotional moments were stabilised again.

* ★ ★ ★

The final week of term slipped by rapidly and the staff room was full of chatter about holiday plans. One or two braver souls were off to the Continent on camping holidays, but most were staying in Britain.

Camping, it seemed, was the holiday of choice for most of the ones with young families. Ian had told some of his friends about their own trip to Anglesey and the inevitable cheeky comments had resulted. But she hadn't minded the friendly teasing and knew that it was going to be wonderful. The chance to spend so much time with the man she loved was exciting, though she wondered what might happen if they didn't see eye to eye about everything.

She told him of her concerns on the way home.

'It would be a miracle if we did,' Ian told her when she voiced her worries. 'How many people have you ever met who agreed on every single thing?'

'You're right of course. We've got so much to look forward to, haven't we? Getting to know each other. Two weddings.'

'Who knows, it might even be three weddings before too long.'

'Maybe. But I'm looking forward to getting to know you a bit first.'

'Come here, you.' He stopped the car at the side of the road and pulled her into his arms and kissed her. He released her and said formally, 'May I introduce myself? Ian Bailey. Bachelor, author and respected teacher.'

'How do you do,' she replied with a smile. 'I'm Lucy Hodges. I look forward to making your acquaintance.'

THE END

ALL TO LOSE

Joyce Johnson

Katie Loveday decides to abandon college to realise her dream of transforming the family home into a country house hotel and spa. With the financial backing of her beloved grandfather the business looks to be a runaway success. But after a tragic accident and the ensuing family squabbles Katie fears she may have to sell her hotel. When she also believes the man she has fallen in love with has designs on her business, the future looks bleak indeed . . .

ERRAND OF LOVE

A. C. Watkins

Jancy Talliman flies halfway around the world to Bungalan, in Australia, to renew an interrupted love affair with Michael Rickwood, who she'd met in London. She remains undaunted on discovering that he's unofficially engaged to Cynthia Meddow, especially given the support of Michael's brother Quentin, and his sister Susan. Jancy settles in a small town nearby. Then as she becomes involved with the townspeople, dam worker Arnulf, and Quentin, Jancy alters the very reason for her long journey south . . .